WITHDRAWN

The
MYSTERIOUS MAKERS
of Shaker Street

SOUNDS
Like
TROUBLE

The Mysterious Makers of Shaker Street
is published by Stone Arch Books,
A Capstone Imprint
1710 Roe Crest Drive
North Mankato, Minnesota 56003
www.mycapstone.com

Cataloging-in-Publication Data is available on the
Library of Congress website.

ISBN: 978-1-4965-4676-0 (library binding)
ISBN: 978-1-4965-4680-7 (paperback)
ISBN: 978-1-4965-4684-5 (eBook PDF)

Summary: When Michael Wilson keeps hearing an
unusual sound at night, he calls on his friends Liv and
Leo to help him figure out what's causing it.

Design Elements: Shutterstock: Master3D, PremiumVector

Designer: Tracy McCabe

Printed in Canada.
010382F17

The
MYSTERIOUS MAKERS
of Shaker Street

SOUNDS Like TROUBLE

by Stacia Deutsch
illustrated by Robin Boyden

STONE ARCH BOOKS
a capstone imprint

CHAPTER ONE

"Last night I heard the strangest noise."

Ten-year-old Michael Wilson was headed home. Walking along with him was his best friend, Leo Hammer, and his cousin, Liv Hernandez.

It was a warm day on Shaker Street. Michael tugged his baseball cap down to shade his dark brown eyes. He said, "It went *whirrrr whirl fzttt.*"

Leo ran a hand over his sandy brown hair. His bangs hung in his face. "Hmm . . . I don't know that one," he said. He readjusted the straps on his heavy backpack, then asked Michael, "Are you sure the *fzttt* was at the end and not in the beginning like *fzttt whirr whirl*?"

"Positive," Michael said. "Why?"

"Well if the *fztt* was at the beginning then I'd say you heard a 1997 Toyota station wagon with a loose fan belt," nine-year-old Leo explained. "But since the *fzztt* is at the end, I'm not sure what that could be." He shrugged. "It's a mystery."

"Mystery?" Liv, who was ten like Michael, was walking ahead of the boys. She spun around and pulled her headphones out of her ears. "I love a mystery!" Pressing a button on her phone, Liv turned off the sound.

"Sorry for ignoring you guys," she added. "I was listening to the last few minutes of *Alien Takeover*. I had to make sure the aliens didn't kidnap the poor old man."

Liv was the only one of them whose parents had gotten her a phone. Leo's dad and Michael's parents agreed that they didn't need one yet. It was a huge bummer.

Michael rolled his eyes at Liv and snorted. "You know that podcast is a hoax, right? There's no scientific proof that extraterrestrial life is real."

"And there's no proof that it's not real," Liv said. She peered over her red vintage glasses frames. "What do you think, Leo?" Liv pinned him with her deep brown stare.

"I —" Leo hesitated. "If there really are aliens, I'd prefer it if they'd stay on their own planet."

"Ah, so you *do* believe in aliens!" Liv exclaimed, grinning. "Leo's the smartest kid at school. Best grades. Best scores. HA!" She faced Michael and put her hands on her hips. "That's all the proof you need," she said. "Aliens exist."

"You're ridiculous," Michael argued. "That's not proof. Besides, Leo's a chicken. If there was a chance that aliens might land on Shaker Street, he'd be at home hiding under the table."

"True," Leo agreed. He tucked his hands into his armpits and clucked. "Bawk, bawk."

Liv insisted, "I'll prove it to you both that the podcast —"

BANG! A firecracker burst over Michael's house. The sparkles glittered in the late afternoon sky.

"Forget the aliens! We gotta go! Now!" Michael shouted at his friends.

They were still near Liv's house at the bottom of Shaker Street. Michael's house was pretty far away, at the dead end at the top of the hill.

The Wilson home was one of the biggest on the block. And it was the tallest.

The old Victorian looked like a skinny purple painted gingerbread house with green icing trim. Above the third floor was a tower room — a turret, Michael's mom called it. There were lots of windows that overlooked the other historic homes of Shaker Street.

Michael saw a flash of light in one of those big windows. Then, as the fireworks faded, a familiar voice boomed through a loudspeaker in the front yard.

"You have five minutes!"

The voice belonged to Michael's grandfather, Henry Wilson Senior.

Michael regretted the day he'd built those small speakers for his grandfather. He'd used two cool-looking tin cigar boxes to hold the wiring. They were supposed to make Grandpa's stereo louder, so his old ears could hear his favorite music. But Grandpa immediately rewired them.

Grandpa thought it was funny that he'd turned the speakers into an announcement system that echoed throughout the entire neighborhood. No one else thought it was funny at all. Especially not Michael. It was embarrassing — for Michael *and* his friends.

"Ticktock," Grandpa called out. His eighty-year-old voice cracked.

"Ugh," Leo groaned, looking up the tall hill. "I hate it when he does this." He tightened his backpack straps for the run. "Someone should call Sheriff Kawasaki."

"She wouldn't do anything," Liv said. "The speakers are annoying, but everyone on Shaker Street loves Grandpa Henry." Henry Senior was Michael's dad's, Henry Junior's, dad. Liv and Michael's moms were sisters, so Liv wasn't related to Henry Senior. Still, she and everyone else called him Grandpa.

Just then the old man called out, "Time's a wastin'."

"Ugh," Leo complained again as they took off running up the hill. "Maybe you could invent some kind of escalator," Leo said to Michael as his breath became heavier. "Or a zip line."

"A zip line that goes up?" Michael asked. He looked at Leo. His friend was slowing down to walk. "That would be against the laws of gravity."

"Some laws need to be broken," Leo said. His face was turning red and sweaty.

They were partway up the hill, nearly at the mustard yellow, weathered house where Leo and his dad rented the second floor.

Nervous that Leo might duck out for a snack and a nap, Michael took his friend's arm. He tugged Leo the rest of the way up the hill, while Liv pushed from behind.

"Come on. We're almost there," Liv said, encouraging Leo to keep going.

"Ticktock," Grandpa's voice cackled through the loudspeaker. "Three minutes and twelve seconds to go. Or else!"

CHAPTER TWO

Michael, Liv, and Leo dashed through the purple house's side gate. They went straight to their Maker Shack Clubhouse.

The clubhouse used to be Grandpa Henry's toolshed. When Michael was old enough, Grandpa gave it to him as a place to hang out and build things. Now Grandpa thought it was fun to lock Michael and his friends out of it with traps.

Michael pulled on the door. To no one's surprise, it was locked.

"What's the situation?" Liv asked, pushing up her glasses. She hovered over Michael's shoulder.

Michael surveyed the locks on the shed door. There was usually only one lock. Michael had the key. Today there were five different ones. They had twisting combination dials instead of keyholes. He twisted the first dial randomly.

"Ticktock," Michael's grandfather called out of an upstairs window. "You have one minute, fifty-eight seconds."

"That's not long enough!" Liv sighed. "The old guy never gives up, does he?"

"We've got this," Michael assured her. He took a closer look.

Michael continued. "So, the first thing I notice is that these combination locks have letters instead of numbers." He turned to Leo. "Can you find any information about this type of lock?"

"You can use my phone," Liv said, rubbing it in that she had one and they didn't.

"Maker Shack Rules," Michael reminded them both.

"Fun killer," Liv muttered, even though she knew the rules. One of them was no phones at the clubhouse. Michael and Leo had made that one up. Since she was the only one with a phone, Liv was outvoted.

But computers were allowed.

"It's okay." Leo swung his backpack to the ground. "I like a big screen." He took out his laptop. "Booting up. Hang on."

While Leo searched the Internet, Liv said, "This whole thing reminds me of the alien podcast! A man called in —" She stopped talking to think for a moment about the story.

Michael looked to Leo with a desperate face. "Hurry."

"You need to rig me some faster Internet!" Leo told Michael.

Liv patiently continued her story. "The caller in the podcast said that aliens had captured him and locked him into their spaceship. They were about to blast off, taking him away from Earth forever, when he realized the code to the lock was made of letters —"

"A cipher!" Leo jumped up and gave Liv a high five. "Michael, it's a code. Each lock takes one letter. They're all connected."

"So we need to figure out a five-letter word to get inside," Liv concluded.

Michael thought about his grandfather and the locks. He realized something important.

While he thought Liv's favorite podcast was silly nonsense, Grandpa loved that same show. "Liv, is there any chance the voice of the caller was familiar?"

"Hmm." Liv bit her bottom lip thoughtfully. "He did have a husky voice that cracked like Grandpa Henry's." She glanced up at Michael's grandfather. He waved at her from the attic window.

"We know it was you!" Michael shouted.

His laugher resonated from the tower.

"Was he really abducted by aliens?" Liv asked Michael.

"Of course not," Michael answered. "He knew you'd be listening to the show. You know Grandpa. It was all part of this set up." With only a minute left, Michael talked fast. "What was the code the aliens used in the story?"

"ALIEN," Liv said.

"Of course," Michael said with a glance at his grandfather's window. It looked like he was dancing in the attic.

"Are you sure he wasn't really abducted?" Liv asked. "They don't let you on the air if your story isn't true."

"It's not true," Michael assured her. "Think about it. Why would aliens want an old guy like him? He's not a very good specimen. They'd be better off with someone like Leo!" Michael laughed as Leo gasped in horror.

With quick fingers, Michael moved each of the lock dials to a letter.

ALIEN

"There." Michael stepped back to see what would happen.

The locks were still locked.

Michael looked at Liv. "Was there anything else interesting in the story?"

"The man, I mean your grandfather, said he had to press a button at the bottom of the last lock. The button opened all the locks. Then, he ran away from the alien's wicked grasp," Liv said.

Sure enough there was a tiny little hole at the bottom of the fifth lock. Michael tried to poke in it with his finger. When that didn't work, he looked for a tool.

"Forty-two seconds!" Grandpa Henry's voice boomed through the loudspeakers.

Michael looked again at the release button. It was bigger than a paper clip. But smaller than a pen cap. He had a idea.

"Leo, give me your shoe." Leo's tennis shoes were always untied.

Leo took off his shoe and handed it to Michael. Michael pressed the small button at the bottom of the last lock with the hard part at the end of the shoelace — the part that's called an aglet. "Come on, ALIEN," he begged.

Click, click, click, click, click.

The locks swung open.

"Wahoo!" Liv shouted.

"We did it!" Michael pushed open the
door to the Maker Shack. Before he went
inside, he waved up at his grandfather.

"You had two seconds to spare!" the old
man shouted. He smiled and gave the kids a
thumbs-up.

"What would have happened if we didn't solve the code?" Liv asked Michael as they entered the dusty clubhouse.

Michael shrugged. "I don't know." He closed the door behind them and said proudly, "We've always solved it."

"Can I have my shoe back?" Leo asked. He held out his hand.

As he sat down to tie up his shoe, Leo noticed a new photo hanging on the wall. "I see you've been decorating," he said.

The picture showed Michael with his mom and dad, Grandpa Henry, Liv, and Leo. They were gathered around a table with a large chocolate cake in the middle. Michael had been adopted as a baby. The picture was taken at his adoption anniversary celebration the week before.

Grandpa had used an antique camera. He attached a self-timer made from a wire hanger and string. That's how he snapped the shot. No fancy "telephone gadgets" were allowed when Grandpa Henry was around.

"Grandpa must have hung it up here," Michael said. He picked up the picture for a better look. There was something lumpy pressed into the back of the frame. Turning it over in his hand, he found a note.

It said:

Someday I'll outsmart you little whippersnappers!

CHAPTER THREE

"Tell us more about the funny noise you heard," Leo said to Michael. "Was it spooky?"

Every corner of the Maker Shack was crammed with Michael's tools and discoveries. There was a chair at a desk. He made it out of a board on top of two brick stacks. Leo took his usual seat at the desk and set up his computer. Michael plopped down on a stool by the workbench. The bench was made from an old door set on top of piled fruit crates.

In the corner was Liv's bright blue beanbag chair. Michael had found it in a dumpster and cleaned it up for her. Liv loved that chair. She'd decorated the entire corner around it. There were leafy plants and a basket for all her magazines.

Liv plopped down in her beanbag with a whoosh. From her basket she picked up a copy of her favorite newsletter. It was called *Suspicious Surprises*. "This month is all about how to chase away ghosts," she said happily. She began skimming the articles while Michael described the sound he'd heard.

"It wasn't a normal sound," he told his friends. "But it wasn't spooky."

Leo hooked up his laptop to a microphone that Michael had found at a yard sale. "Make the noise again. I can search the web for what it might be," Leo said.

Leo typed commands into his laptop, which was another of Michael's Maker Space projects. The laptop had been Leo's dad's boss's and was headed for the trash. Michael had rescued it and given it new life.

"*Whirrrr whirl fzttt,*" Michael said into the microphone, repeating the sound a few times. Leo made a recording. Then Leo scanned an online database.

Liv set down the newsletter. "You say you only hear this mysterious noise at night?" she asked Michael.

"Yeah. Every night for the past week." He hadn't told his friends at first because he thought it was just an animal or something like that. But as the noisy nights went on, he changed his mind. Michael decided it was definitely something more unusual than a stray cat or a raccoon.

Michael said, "Last night, I woke up Mom and Dad so they could listen. But they didn't think it was weird. And Grandpa can't hear anything after he takes out his hearing aids."

"So what do you want to do?" Liv asked. Her eyes followed Michael as he paced around the shed.

"Phase One is see if Leo can identify the noise," Michael said. He looked over Leo's laptop screen. The words *NO MATCH* were blinking rapidly in bright red letters as the computer continued to search. "Phase Two is to go out at midnight tonight to investigate."

"Yay for Phase Two!" Liv cheered.

Leo moaned. "Come on, baby." He patted his laptop with a loving hand. "Give me what you've got." *NO MATCH* continued to light up the screen.

"We're going to need supplies," Michael told Liv.

"What are we making?" she asked. She looked over the Maker Shack bins of wires and electrodes and metal cases and wheels. All the bins were marked in pen with labels declaring what was inside.

"A sound amplifier," Michael said. He pulled down boxes from the shelves and piled them next to Leo at the workstation. "Human ears are limited. To hear what's going on, we need to make the noise louder and clearer."

Liv raised her eyes. "I think there's an app for that . . . Come on, Michael. Let's use my phone. Just this once."

In response, Michael clicked his tongue and pointed over Leo's head.

There, posted in the center of the longest wall, were the rules for Mysterious Makers of Shaker Street.

The large piece of cardboard had come from a refrigerator box flap. It read:

The Mysterious Makers
of Shaker Street Promise

1) We turn old things into new things.

2) We don't use new things if we can use old things.

Leo had scribbled at the bottom:

Computers are okay.

Liv had added:

Phones are okay if zombies attack. Call me!

The last line read:

This contract is legally binding.

The last part was also Leo's addition. His dad was a lawyer, and he wanted the document to sound official, even if it was made out of cardboard.

Liv, Michael, and Leo had all signed the agreement in permanent pen.

"Oh well." Liv sighed. "How's the computer search, Leo?"

"I got nothin'." Leo's computer search had come to an end. There was no matching sound.

With a frown, he reported, "I was hoping it was the call of a rare bird. Maybe the happy yip of a fuzzy bunny rabbit." Leo knew what was coming next. "I guess we're going with Phase Two?" he asked.

"Yes! Phase Two!" Liv jumped around clapping her hands.

Michael began opening bin lids, looking under box tops, and piling supplies on the counter. "This is going to take a while," he said, pinching his lips together. "We need to stay up late, so . . ." He raised an eyebrow. "I'm sure my parents will agree — you're both invited to a sleepover."

"A *creepover* is more like it," Leo said with a grunt. "We're spending the night listening to some spooky noise."

"You don't have to stay," Liv said. Her cheeks were flushed with excitement. "You could go home."

"I know," Leo said. But as scared as he might be of what they might find, Leo was first and foremost a loyal friend. Liv and Michael both knew he'd never leave. Especially when there was a mystery to solve.

CHAPTER FOUR

Leo slept over all the time. His dad was fine with it as long as Leo called before bed to say good night.

Liv's parents were divorced. Her mom lived on Shaker Street. Her dad lived a few blocks away. Since Liv and Michael were cousins, they often stayed at each other's houses.

"Since I'm staying here, Mom's going to have a movie marathon with CoCo," Liv said when she hung up the phone. CoCo was five and liked shows about musical animals. "There's no such thing as a singing bear," Liv said, rolling her eyes. "That's so unrealistic!"

Michael and Leo laughed. Then they went into the big house for dinner.

A few hours later, the three of them returned to the clubhouse. Michael had most of what he needed for the amplifier laid out on the worktable.

"Do you want me to look up how to make one?" Leo asked.

"Nah," Michael said. "I'm sure we'll figure it out." He already had a few ideas of where to start.

He picked up an old tape recorder. It was a small silver box with a speaker on the front. A mini tape cassette went into a slot. A thick gray button played the tape, which was a rectangle about the size of two thumbs side-by-side.

"Wow," Leo said, looking at the recorder. "Where'd you get that?" They always tried to find parts for the things they made. Dumpsters and garage sales were the best places for Maker Shack treasures.

"This was my mom's," Michael said. "When she started selling houses, she used it to record her customers talking about what they wanted. Then she'd help them find the perfect place."

"She's the best house seller on Shaker Street," Leo said. "But I'm glad she's using her phone now." He smiled.

"I know," Michael said happily. "If she was still using a tape recorder, we wouldn't have one!"

Michael set the recorder on the workbench. "I found it in a drawer of junk," he said.

He got a pair of earphones, the kind with the long wire. The recorder had a speaker, but the sound would be clearer — and more private — through the earphones.

Liv was going through a box of small microphones that could be plugged into the tape recorder.

"If we can hear sounds from around the neighborhood," she held up the smallest microphone in the bin, "do you think we could amplify sounds from outer space too?" She raised the microphone to her mouth and said, "Anyone out there?"

"You can't hear something that doesn't exist," Michael said.

He snatched the microphone and was about to plug it into the tape recorder. But stopped. He looked for some wire. It would be better to put the microphone on a long wire. That way the recorder could be near the computer, and the microphone could pick up sounds that were outside and further away.

He measured out some extra wire. Attached it. Then plugged in the microphone. There were two input slots. He put earphones in the second hole.

"It's ready." Michael stuck a small cassette tape into the recorder. He held the whole thing in the palm of his hand. "Let's try this out."

44

"I'll go into the yard," Liv suggested. "I'll start pretty far away. See if you can hear me. I'll move around to test it."

"When we find you, I'll run your voice through the computer. If we use a GPS, maybe we can track where you are," Leo suggested. His fingers were already typing commands into the laptop. "It's like hide-and-seek for Liv."

"If you can't find me, shout out 'Olly, Olly Oxen Free!'" Liv laughed. She left the clubhouse and disappeared through the gate toward the front of the house.

Michael set the tape recorder on the workbench. He stretched out the microphone wire, pointing the microphone toward the place he last saw Liv. He stopped the motor on the recorder, so there'd be no interference. Then Michael put the earbud in his ear.

"Can you hear her?" Leo asked. "Once you get sound, we'll put the earbud next to the computer. I can record the sound and get an ID."

Michael closed his eyes. "I hear . . . breathing."

"Oh, sorry," Leo said, slamming a hand over his mouth. With hand motions, he asked Michael, *Can you hear anything now?*

Michael shook his head.

Leo let out his breath. "Whew," he said. "I thought I might explode."

"Impossible," Michael assured him, then listened some more. He shook his head. "It's not working."

"The microphone isn't strong enough to reach Liv," Leo said. "She has to come in closer."

"Not yet," Michael said. His eyes flitted around the room, searching his supplies. "We just need a way to get the sound to come through louder."

"An antenna?" Leo suggested. "What else makes things louder?" He cupped his ear with his hand and joked, "Eh? I can't hear you."

"That's it! Good thinking, Leo!" Michael exclaimed.

"You're welcome," Leo said even though he didn't know what he'd done.

Michael ran to get a box of poster board left over from school projects. He took out a piece of fluorescent pink board, recycled from Liv's science fair project, and rolled it into a cone. Then he put the microphone in the cone.

"It's like how your cupped hand focuses the sound," he explained.

Sticking the cone and microphone outside the window, he could clearly hear Liv now.

"Hang on," Leo said, typing on the keyboard. "Pass the earphone. I'll pinpoint her location in a second."

"Forget it," Michael said with a laugh. "I know where she is."

He turned up the amplifier's volume so they both could hear from one bud.

"Were you scared? Did they try to shoot at you with their laser eyes?" Liv was rattling on and on.

Michael looked to Leo and said with a chuckle, "She's on the front porch with Grandpa."

"I'm sure he'll keep her busy with stories until midnight," Leo said, pulling two remote controllers out of his backpack. "Want to play video games?"

Michael checked the clock. It was three hours until midnight. They had tons of time. "Sure," he said, taking the red controller. "What do you want to play?"

Leo winked and said, "Let's shoot space aliens."

CHAPTER FIVE

At exactly midnight, Michael and Leo tiptoed out of Michael's room. Liv was in the guest room at the end of the hall. She snuck out and met them at the bottom of the stairs.

"This way." Michael led his friends out the back door to the Maker Shack Clubhouse. "Whew," he said, noting that his grandfather hadn't messed with the locks again . . . yet.

They entered the clubhouse and Liv picked up the sound amplifier.

"I really wish we could hear aliens," she said. She held the cone, with the microphone in it, toward the sky and shouted, "Anyone out there?"

"*Shhh . . .*" Michael put a finger over his lips. "We don't want to alert whoever's making the sound."

"Or wake up Michael's parents," Leo said as the computer booted up.

Michael took the listening device. He put the earbud next to the laptop and turned up the volume.

"There!" Michael said, looking at Leo's computer screen. A little green light was bouncing all around. That meant the strange sound was coming through.

"Can you figure out where it's coming from?" he asked Leo.

Leo began to use a GPS to locate the source. A minute later he said, "It's too far away." He leaned back in his chair and said, "Since we can't find out what it is, I think we should go back to bed . . . where it's safe."

"*Whirrrr whirl fzttt.*" Liv imitated the noise. They were all hearing it clearly now. "Sorry, Leo. I think it's coming from somewhere on Shaker Street. Let's walk slowly down the hill to find out exactly which house."

"No thanks," Leo insisted. "We should stay right here. When there's trouble, it's always the little, slow guy who gets caught."

"True," Liv told him, winking at Michael. "But we'll rescue you. Don't worry."

"Ugh." Leo groaned.

"We're gonna need a few things." Michael began pulling bins off the shelves.

He grabbed a backpack from a low shelf. "This is our new Maker Shack Maker Sack," he explained. He set the old, dirty, dark blue pack on the worktable. "I found it in a trash can behind school. I don't get why someone tossed it out."

"Uh, because there's a hole in the bottom," Liv said. She stuck her hand all the way through and wiggled her fingers at Michael.

Michael replied, "It's still good." He handed her a roll of heavy-duty silver duct tape.

Liv smiled. "I'll fix it." She taped up the bottom of the bag while Michael ran around the shed and Leo packed up his laptop. When the backpack was ready, Liv wrote "Maker Sack" on the front in strips of the silver sticky tape.

Michael then stuffed the Maker Sack with things he thought they might need: a suction cup, a wire hanger, alligator clips (which are wire with clips on the end), some extra long pieces of wire, a penny, a few nails, and three small LED bulbs.

"We need one more thing," Michael said as they snuck out of the clubhouse. He took one of Grandpa's blasting speakers from the front porch and stuck it in the Maker Sack.

"I'll put everything back tomorrow," Michael told his friends as he slipped the backpack over his shoulders.

"Maybe not Grandpa Henry's speaker," Leo suggested with a grin. "No one would mind if it disappeared."

"He'll just make a new one," Michael assured Leo. "Even louder."

Michael helped Leo slip a strange contraption around his neck. It was made of bungee cords and an old man's leather briefcase. The briefcase hung like a portable table for Leo to put his computer on, so he could walk and type at the same time. Using a Wi-Fi booster from the clubhouse, Leo could keep his laptop and the GPS system running all the way down Shaker Street.

Liv had the amplifier. She listened to the sound, then tried to guess which way to go.

Leo had the GPS. Running the *whirring* sound through his computer, Leo could figure out which way it was coming from. "This direction," he said, leading them.

Streetlights lit their path. They passed Michael's neighbor to the left. Liv pointed the amplifier's cone toward the house on the right.

They still weren't close to the noise that Michael heard. It was still too far away. Slowly, they made their way down the street.

"Oof!" Liv stopped so suddenly that Leo bumped her in the back. "Oof," he said again, stumbling into the yard of a two-story, plain-looking, beige house with a *FOR SALE* sign in the yard.

Liv reached out to steady Leo with one hand. "The sound's definitely coming from this one," she reported.

Michael took the amplifier and made sure it was directed at the house. Then he checked that the earphone was sending the sounds through Leo's laptop.

The three of them listened quietly to the *whirrrr whirl fzttt* sound while Leo scanned the noise.

"It's definitely here," Leo said. There was a shiver in his voice. "But the sound isn't coming from inside the house." He clicked a few buttons on his laptop. "I've looked at the GPS coordinates. And checked the math three times. The equations check out. That sound is coming from under the house."

CHAPTER SIX

"My mom's actually selling this house," Michael said as they walked slowly around toward the backyard. "No one has lived here for months."

"Weird," Liv remarked, wrinkling her eyebrows. "So what do you think is in there, Michael? Ghosts? Zombies? Huge, genetically modified rats?"

"A person." Michael said flatly, picking up a piece of paper near the fence.

He held up the burger wrapper and added, "Just one hungry human being."

Liv shook her head, then her eyes widened. "Maybe it's a vampire! If it's a vampire, we shouldn't go in. We don't have the right supplies."

"A vampire who likes cheeseburgers?" Michael asked. "I don't think so."

"Maybe he ordered the meat rare?" Liv said, acting insulted that Michael would even ask.

"Vampires? Rare meat? I gotta go," Leo said. He started to disconnect himself from the laptop carrying case. "I hear my dad calling."

Michael chuckled. "He's asleep." To prove it, he pointed the sound amplifier toward Leo's house. "I can hear him snoring."

Leo's shoulders slumped. "We cannot break into this house. Nope. No way," he said. "Sheriff Kawasaki would be here in a flash. I can't have an arrest on my college record."

"You're only nine years old," Michael said, raising an eyebrow.

"I know," Leo said. "I like to think ahead."

"I'll admit this is scary, but I'm sure it's a person in there. A normal person." Michael told Leo.

"We don't have to break in," Liv told Leo. She leaned over the side fence and pointed. "The back door's open."

"That seems bad —" Leo began. But before he finished his sentence, Liv and Michael were through the gate and into the open door.

From inside the house, Liv leaned her head through a small open window. Soft white curtains billowed around her face. She pushed them back and whispered, "Bring the computer, Leo. Hurry."

Leo groaned. "First thing tomorrow, I'm getting new friends," he said. Tightening his computer carrier straps, he headed into the abandoned house.

"We don't need the amplifier anymore," Michael said. He stopped in the small kitchen to put it in his Maker Sack. The glow of a streetlight gave them enough light to see.

"Look at that," he told the others. There was a hole in the floor behind a narrow staircase. The stairs went up. The hole went down.

"Oh, boy," Leo shivered and sighed.

The *whirrrr whirl fzttt* sound had stopped. "Maybe whoever, or whatever, is making that noise went home for the night?" he said.

"We're checking it out," Liv told him. "Leave the laptop here. We'll get it on the way back."

Reluctantly, Leo took off his computer carrier and set it on the kitchen counter next to a roll of papers, rubber banded like a tube. He pointed at the papers.

"I wonder what those are," Liv said with a shrug. She started to unroll them when the *whirrrr whirl fzttt* sound started up again. It came from underneath them and echoed through the kitchen.

Liv put down the papers, and they hurried to examine the hole in the floor. There was a rope ladder swinging down from where they stood. It was impossible to see the bottom.

Michael stepped onto the ladder to go down first. He ran a finger over his lips, reminding Leo and Liv to be quiet. When he reached the bottom, Michael shook the ladder as a signal for the next person to start.

Liv came down.

When it was Leo's turn, he grumbled softly the whole way.

At the bottom, it was completely dark. Michael reached out and gently touched Leo on the shoulder. Liv's hand brushed Michael's, so he knew they were all together.

The three of them snuck, silent as mice, through the tunnel. Michael was in the lead. He wished he'd thought to bring a flashlight in his Maker Sack.

He'd brought LED bulbs, but that just seemed silly now. What was he thinking? Bulbs with no battery?

Michael decided that when they got home he'd put a permanent flashlight in the Maker Sack — just in case.

For now, it was too late. They couldn't see, but he knew they were getting closer to the source of the noise. The *whirrrr whirl fzttt* was getting louder.

They went forward, very slowly. The tunnel was much longer than Michael expected. They walked for a while.

In the distance, Michael could make out the end of the tunnel. Slivers of light shone through cracks in the wall to reveal a shape looming at the end.

It looked like a long tube with sharp blades on the front. Almost like a drill with a shovel. Michael had never seen anything like that. It was so strange looking. He wanted a closer look.

Edging forward, Michael was leading his friends toward the odd machine when suddenly, he saw movement in the shadows.

Michael gasped. It was a man.

The man turned toward Michael.

Michael stopped quickly and ducked down. They needed to stay out of sight. He put up a hand as a signal to tell Liv and Leo to stop too. But the space was too dark. Liv hit Michael's hand and bounced back. Then, Leo smacked into Liv and yelped, "Oof!"

The man's voice rang out. "Who's there?" The *whirrrr whirl fzttt* stopped, and suddenly a flashlight shined their way. "Who's there?" the voice shouted again.

In a hard whisper, the man said, "Ghosts be gone," which Michael thought was very odd.

"Be gone!" the man shouted in a louder voice.

A clanging noise began. It sounded like a spoon hitting a metal pot.

"Run!" Michael whispered to his friends. He pushed at Liv in the darkness. "To the ladder!"

No one needed to tell Leo. Michael could hear him climbing up. He must have taken off the instant the man shouted at them.

All three Makers got up the rope ladder in seconds, but the man from the tunnel was right behind them.

"In here!" Liv motioned toward a large pantry in the kitchen. There was plenty of room to hide inside. She closed the door behind Leo.

"Wait." Leo ducked back out.

He grabbed his laptop from the counter and took the roll of papers. "In case we need to hit someone with it," he said, swinging the tube like a bat.

Again, Liv closed the door behind them. They didn't dare to breathe as the man entered the kitchen.

His heavy footsteps clicked against the tile. He grumbled something that sounded like, "Haunted," then disappeared out of the room. The footsteps faded.

Liv cracked open the pantry door. Moonlight from the window lit the space. She made sure the man was gone, then she looked around their hiding place.

"For an empty house," Liv said in a whisper, "there sure is a lot of food in the pantry."

"I wonder what he's up to," Michael said to the others. They were keeping their voices soft, just in case the man heard them. Michael searched through the bags and found chips, dry pasta, and a basket of lemons. "Looks like he's been living here," he said.

"I bet he goes away in the day and comes back at night," Leo told Michael. "He can't risk that your mom might come in to show people the house."

"Who's gonna buy this house now? There's a hole in the floor," Liv reminded them.

Micheal considered the hole for a moment. "He must cover it," he concluded. "It would be easy to hide the hole with a wood board and some carpet."

Liv took the tube of papers from Leo. She removed the rubber band and spread the papers out on the kitchen counter, where the moonlight was bright enough to read by.

After studying the drawings for a long moment, Liv gasped.

"I know what he's doing," she said, voice rising. "He's making a tunnel from this house all the way to this building at the end of the street." With a long finger, she traced the path between the buildings. "Look! The tunnel ends in the Shaker Street Bank's vault." She tapped the plans. "He's going to rob the bank!"

CHAPTER SEVEN

"We have to stop him," Michael said, pacing the kitchen. The *whirrrr whirl fzttt* sound had begun again below them, and now Michael knew what it meant.

The thief was back at work in the tunnel. He was running the machine. And Michael knew exactly what that contraption did.

The *whirrrr* was the motor of a huge digging drill. Those were the sharp blades he'd seen.

The *whirl* was a scoop removing dirt and setting it aside. That was the shovel he'd noticed.

The *fzttt* was the machine resetting over and over again. It would dig a little, then dump out the dirt. Reset and do it again.

He'd seen slivers of light. That meant the tunnel was almost at the bank.

The drill was so loud, Michael and his friends could walk and talk normally. The man wouldn't be able to hear them.

"How are *we* going to stop the crook?" Leo asked. "We gotta call the sheriff."

"The man might run away," Liv said. "We're here now." She put her hand on Leo's arm. "We can do this on our own."

Leo released a heavy breath, but he didn't argue.

"Fine," he said, giving in. "What's the plan? We can't see in the tunnel. How are we going to stop someone we can't see?"

Michael began dumping things out of his Maker Sack onto the countertop. "I've got this," he muttered. "Liv, grab a couple lemons from the pantry."

She gave a sideways confused look to Leo but grabbed two lemons.

"Three would be better," Michael said. "But let's try this." He stuck pennies in each lemon. Then he put nails in the opposite side of the fruit.

"I know what he's doing," Leo told Liv, quietly so as not to interrupt Michael's focus or to attract the man under the house. "Batteries are made of two metals in an acid solution."

"The nail is one metal," Liv said, watching Michael connect alligator clips to the nails. "The penny is copper, so that's a second metal."

Michael connected a nail from one lemon to a penny in the other. Then he connected the other penny to the little LED bulb he'd put in the Maker Sack. And from the second lemon, he connected a nail to the bulb.

When the circuit was complete, the bulb began to glow!

It was faint, but the lemon light was going to be just enough. They could see where they were going.

"Cool," Liv said, admiring the "flashlight" that Michael had made.

He grabbed four more lemons and made two more lights — one for each of them.

Then Michael said, "Let's go catch a bad guy."

Michael put the Maker Sack on his back.

Leo booted his laptop up for a second, typed into the keyboard, then shut it all back down.

"If he escapes," Leo said, "I don't want him taking my laptop with him." He set the computer on a shelf in the pantry and blew it a kiss. "See you soon," he said and shut the door.

They made their way back down the ladder. Liv stopped them at the bottom. "Uh, Michael. The lights are great, but how are we going to catch this guy?"

In the glow of the lemon lights, Michael thought they all looked spooky. They looked like ghosts — which of course, didn't actually exist.

Michael had a practical idea. "We'll get him to chase us into the street."

"Then what?" Leo asked.

Michael had already considered that. "Then Leo goes to the neighbor to call the sheriff," he said.

"Already done," Leo said with a grin. "I emailed her a minute ago. I told her to come to the middle of Shaker Street as soon as possible. I said that she'd find a crook there. Luckily, she checks her email regularly!"

"I guess we better get this thief outside then," Michael said, glad that Leo and Liv were with him. He needed his friends. "The problem is that the tunnel is a dead end on his side," Michael explained. "We have to make him run toward us because he has to go up the ladder."

Liv raised her light to her face, making her look extra spooky. "That's too dangerous. Leo might get caught."

The way she said it, Michael knew she was teasing, but it was a real possibility. "We need the thief to leave the house without catching us," Michael said.

"How are we going to do that?" Leo asked.

"I know. We'll scare him out. He's afraid of ghosts," Liv told them.

"What are you talking about?" Michael said a bit too loud. He lowered his voice, and simply grunted, "Huh?"

Liv explained, "Remember that article I read earlier in the *Suspicious Surprises* newsletter? The one about scaring ghosts away? The article suggested banging on a pan with a wooden spoon."

She smiled and continued, "I think the thief read that same article. That's what that sound was after he yelled at us. He thought we were ghosts."

"He even said, 'Haunted,'" Leo said with a smile. His teeth looked yellow in the faintly glowing light.

"We just have to convince him the house — and the tunnel — are really, truly haunted," Liv said with confidence. "He'll be so scared that he'll run into the street and straight into Sheriff Kawasaki's handcuffs."

"So now we have to figure out how to scare him . . . ," Leo said. He looked to Michael. "What else do you have in that sack?"

Michael grinned, putting the bag on the floor of the tunnel and opening the zipper. "I've got exactly what we need."

"If I take apart the earbuds and attach the wires to Grandpa's speaker . . . ," Michael muttered to himself as he worked in the glow of all three lemon lights, "I can plug the speaker into the tape recorder. Instead of a sound amplifier, it'll blast sound like a PA system."

Suddenly the *whirrrr whirl fzttt* sound stopped.

"Oh, no! I think he's taking a break," Liv whispered to Michael. "Are you done? We gotta get out of here!"

"I'm done." Michael pushed past Leo to reach for the ladder. "Hurry. Let's go upstairs. Just in case he's going to the kitchen for a snack. We can hide somewhere until he's back in the tunnel."

They all agreed.

Very quietly, Michael stepped rung to rung until he reached the top. Liv followed.

"Oof!" That was the sound of Leo falling off the ladder. "I missed a rung!" He shouted as he scampered up again.

The voice from the tunnel started to boom, "Who's there? Is anyone there?"

A few moments later, Leo shouted, "Help! He's got me!"

CHAPTER EIGHT

"The rest of you, get back down here now," the thief threatened. "Or else."

"No one ever says what 'or else' means," Liv told Michael with a groan. "Why can't it be 'Or else we'll have cookies?'"

"Help!" Leo shouted again. "*Heeeellllp!*"

Liv turned to Michael. "Quick, can you make it sound like there's a ghost in the tunnel?"

"On it." Michael pressed record on the tape recorder so that the microphone would blast sound through the speaker. *"Oooh, oooh . . . ,"* he started.

"Is that seriously what you think a ghost sounds like?" Liv took the tape recorder and microphone from Michael's hands. She left him holding the speaker.

Then Liv started screaming in a high-pitched wail. "You have disturbed my burial grounds!" Her voice blasted through the speaker.

Michael leaned over the tunnel to let the speaker hang down. "It'll echo," he told Liv. "Keep going."

"Let the boy go . . . ," she cried out. "Or else!" There was no response from down in the tunnel.

Liv put down the microphone. She asked Michael, "What are we going to do?"

"We gotta save Leo," Michael said. He was starting to panic. "This is all my fault!"

Liv bit her lip, then said, "I have an idea. Can you get those fruit lights going again?"

"Of course," Michael confirmed. He checked the connections and handed Liv a lemon light.

Liv looked around the house. "I need the curtains," she said, dashing over to the back door. When Liv came back a second later, she was wearing a curtain over her head. She stuck a fruit light underneath it so the curtain glowed.

"Wow," Michael said, feeling goose bumps pop out all over his arms. "If I believed in ghosts, I'd swear you were one."

"I'm going into the tunnel," she said, mustering up her courage. "You can be my voice."

"I can't," Michael told her. "I'm a terrible ghost." To prove it, he said, "Oooh . . ." one more time. He grabbed his backpack and pulled out several very long pieces of wire. "I'm going to rig the microphone so you can take it with you," Michael told her.

With fast fingers, he twisted wires together and attached them to the microphone. The cord was now long enough that Liv could carry it wherever she went. He'd stay back, slowly unwind the wire for Liv, and hold the speaker so the sound would echo through the whole tunnel.

Michael helped Liv carry the curtains and the lemon light down the ladder. When they reached the bottom, he said, "Go save Leo."

She nodded, then began to pretend she was a ghost. "Now you have angered me," she said in her scary voice. "I am coming to get you. Watch out . . ."

Michael could see the glow from Liv's curtain costume as she disappeared into the darkness. Then he heard the banging. The spoon was slamming against the pot. He knew the thief was scared.

"Away, evil spirit," the man shouted.

"Liv, get back here," Michael whispered into the shadows. "I think this is too dangerous."

She didn't answer. He didn't think she could hear him over the sound of the speaker.

"You cannot escape my wrath!" Liv shouted into the microphone. Her voice crackled.

"I knew this house was haunted!"
The thief was banging his pot wildly and
screaming, "*Aaaaaaauuuuuuugh!*"

The thief knocked Liv over on his way to
the ladder. Michael ducked to the side, just
in time. The man rushed past him, climbed
the ladder, and ran screaming out the front
door of the house.

The police sirens were loud. Michael knew the sheriff had gotten Leo's email. She was there in time. The crook was captured.

Liv appeared back through the tunnel. "Good ghost," Michael told her. He peered into the darkness. "Where's Leo?"

She took off her costume and they went in search of their friend. They found him at the end of the tunnel. He was sitting against the farthest wall, behind the digging equipment.

"Leo?" Michael was worried the thief had hurt his friend. "You okay?"

"I-I-I," Leo stuttered. "I-I-I . . ."

Liv sat down on the floor next to him. "What happened?" she asked.

"I saw a ghost!" Leo jumped up. "It was wearing white and speaking in this spooky voice. And its face glowed!"

Leo was shaking as he pointed down the tunnel toward the exit. "It was right there!" he said.

Liv started to laugh. Michael laughed too.

"What?!" Leo insisted. "Don't make fun of me. I know what I saw, and it was terrifying."

"It was me," Liv told him with a smile. "I'm the ghost."

"No way!" Leo said. He refused to believe his friends.

"Let the boy go . . . or else," Liv said in her ghostly voice. "I used a lemon light under the house curtains." She held up the little light that was now illuminating the tunnel.

Leo studied Liv's face for a long moment, then nodded. "And her voice went through your speaker?" he asked Michael.

"Yep," Michael admitted.

Michael was sure that Leo would be mad that he'd gotten caught in their trap to scare the thief, but instead he started to giggle. "There's no such thing as ghosts," Leo said, feeling better.

"Right," Michael said.

"At least not in this house," Liv corrected them.

They all followed Liv's lemon light to the ladder and up into the kitchen.

Sheriff Kawasaki was standing by the pantry. She held Leo's laptop in one hand and the thief's plans for the tunnel in the other.

The sheriff was young with shoulder-length black hair and fierce eyes that could scare a crook.

Her family had moved to Shaker Street from Japan when she was a baby. She grew up on this street and now was sworn to protect it.

"Does this belong to you?" she asked, holding out the laptop to Leo.

"Uh-huh." He took it, nodding sheepishly.

Michael wondered what she'd say to them. Were they in trouble?

"We've taken Mr. Slater into custody," she told the kids. "He was a tunnel engineer who decided to start robbing banks. For years, he's been tunneling under houses all over the world. Now, thanks to all of you, he's going to jail."

"Awesome!" Liv cheered, raising her hand to high-five the boys.

The sheriff stopped her.

"Not so fast, young lady." The sheriff had her intense eyes pinned on Liv's face. "You shouldn't be here." She looked from Michael to Leo and back to Liv. "It's late. You're trespassing and breaking and entering. Plus you stole curtains and lemons that didn't belong to you." At that, Liv set her lemon light on the counter.

"Give me one reason why I shouldn't arrest you," the sheriff said, looking from Michael to Liv and back to Leo. "If you can convince me, I'll let you go."

CHAPTER NINE

Liv plopped down into the beanbag chair at the Maker Space Clubhouse. "I can't believe she let us go!"

Michael took a seat at the worktable, while Leo plugged in his computer.

"She didn't let us go, exactly," Leo said. "Your mom, my dad, Michael's parents, and even Grandpa Henry are in house having a 'conference.'" He made air quotes with his fingers.

"Conference schmonference." Liv leaned her head back into the beanbag. "We aren't in jail," she said. "And I'm telling you, the sheriff was happy for our help."

"She didn't seem happy though," Michael said. He imitated the way she sideways stared at them with one dark eye. "In fact, I think it was the opposite."

"Nah." Liv yawned. "She was happy. Without us, Mr. Slater would have robbed the Shaker Street Bank and gotten away with it." She stretched her arms above her head and yawned again. "Catching crooks is hard work."

"Yes it is," Sheriff Kawasaki said as she entered the clubhouse. "And that's why catching crooks should be left to the sheriff." She pointed at herself.

Liv went to stand beside the boys as all the adults came into the clubhouse. It was crowded in there with so many people.

Michael gave a small wave to his parents, who shook their heads as if to say, "What were you thinking?!"

Liv's mom had a flat expression. It was as if she expected to discover Liv sneaking around an old house at night.

Leo's dad looked tired. He stood closest to the sheriff, with his eyes on Leo. Leo shrugged. His dad shrugged back. In some ways, it looked to Michael as if Mr. Hammer was proud of Leo for overcoming his fears to help catch a thief.

The only one smiling was Grandpa Henry. His grin stretched ear to ear. "Now that's my boy!" he cheered.

All the parents instantly glared at him. "What?" he asked innocently. "These kids are heroes." Michael would have laughed if Sheriff Kawasaki wasn't giving him that evil side-eye.

"Your parents and I have agreed," the sheriff began. "Going after a thief on your own wasn't smart. But," she went on, "it turned out to be helpful."

"Heroes, I tell ya," Grandpa cut in, raising a victory fist.

The sheriff shot him a warning look.

He stepped back.

"So," she turned her hand toward all the adults, "we have agreed — no one is grounded. No one is in trouble."

Michael looked at his friends. That was not what he expected.

"And no one ever does anything else like this ever again."

That was what he expected.

Liv was the first to agree. "Got it," she said.

"Understood." Leo hugged his dad.

"No more sneaking around at night," Michael promised, going to stand between his parents.

The sun was rising when Leo, Liv, and Michael followed the group back into the big house. They were going to sleep for a few hours, then make something new in the clubhouse.

"I told you the sheriff was glad we helped," Liv said as they stood together in the hallway, before going to separate rooms. "Did you see her wink?"

"What wink?" Michael and Leo said at the same time.

"The one she gave us just before she left," Liv said. "The one that meant we should help her out solving crimes whenever we want."

"What are you talking about?" Leo asked Liv. He wrinkled his eyebrows and stared at her.

"I didn't see anything," Michael said. "In fact, I think we all promised *not* to snoop around Shaker Street anymore."

"You weren't listening." Liv shook her head. "You need to hear words that aren't said. Sheriff Kawasaki just hired the Makers of Shaker Street to be on the lookout for anything suspicious. It's our job."

"Are you sure?" Michael asked. There was no way . . .

"Positive," Liv said, opening the door to the guest room and giving a big yawn. "We start tomorrow."

YOU CAN BE A MYSTERIOUS MAKER TOO:

LEO'S LOUD AMPLIFIER

Things to find:

- Earbuds with wire attached
- Microphone
- Small tape recorder
- Cassette tape for the recorder
- Tag board

TRY THIS!
If you add foil to the inside of the tag board tube, the reflective surface should increase the sound even further.

Directions:

1. Put the tape in the recorder.
2. Plug the earbuds into the correct jack.
3. Plug the microphone into the other jack.
4. Press the record button and the pause buttons together.
5. Create a cone from the tag board. Tape it together.
6. Tape the microphone into the cone.
7. Turn up the volume. You should be able to hear the sounds coming from the microphone through the earbuds.

MICHAEL'S TAPE RECORDER MEGAPHONE

(Continued from steps 1-7)

8. Exchange the earbuds with a portable speaker.
9. Press record and pause together.
10. Use the microphone. The sound should come out the speaker.
11. Make your own ghostly growls.

LIV'S LEMON LIGHT

Things to find:

- 2 Lemons
- 2 Pennies (must be before 1982 so there is enough copper content) or two copper wires
- 2 Galvanized nails
- 3 Test lead alligator clips (a clip with a wire attached to either end)
- LED bulb

Directions

1. Put a nail and a penny into the skin of each lemon. Make sure there is space between the nail and the penny.
2. Attach a test lead alligator clip from the penny on one lemon to the nail on the other.
3. Attach a clip from one nail to the LED.
4. Attach a clip from one penny to the other LED.
5. If your light isn't glowing, try adding more lemons to the chain.

ABOUT THE AUTHOR

Stacia Deutsch is the author of more than two hundred children's books, including the eight-book, award-winning, chapter book series *Blast to the Past*. Her résumé also includes *Nancy Drew and the Clue Crew*, *The Boxcar Children*, and *Mean Ghouls*. Stacia has also written junior movie tie-in novels for summer blockbuster films, including *Batman*, *The Dark Knight* and *The New York Times* best sellers *Cloudy with a Chance of Meatballs Jr.* and *The Smurfs*. She earned her MFA from Western State where she currently teaches fiction writing.

ABOUT THE ILLUSTRATOR

Robin Boyden works as an illustrator, writer, and designer and is based in Bristol, England. He has first-class BA honors in illustration from the University of Falmouth and an MA in Art and Design from the University of Hertfordshire. He has worked with a number of clients in the editorial and publishing sectors including Bloomsbury Publishing, *The Phoenix* comic, BBC, *The Guardian*, *The Times*, Oxford University Press, and Usborne Publishing.

GLOSSARY

abduct (ab-DUKT)—kidnap someone

amplifier (AM-pluh-fye-ur)—a piece of equipment that makes a sound louder

amplify (AM-pli-fye)—to make something louder or stronger

contraption (kuhn-TRAP-shuhn)—a strange or odd device or machine

cipher (SYE-fer)—a message in code

database (DAY-tuh-bayss)—a collection of information that is organized and stored in a computer

electrodes (i-LEK-trodes)—points through which an electric current can flow into or out of a device or substance

extraterrestrial (ek-struh-tuh-RESS-tree-uhl)—coming from outer space

interference (in-tur-FIHR-uhnss)—something that interrupts sound or vision so that it does not work properly

specimen (SPESS-uh-muhn)—a sample used to stand for a whole group

TALK WITH YOUR FELLOW MAKERS!

1. The Mysterious Makers of Shaker Street have several club rules, including no phones. How would the book have been different if they would have used Liv's phone?

2. The Mysterious Makers think of themselves as inventors. What are some characteristics of good inventors? Do the Makers have these characteristics?

3. At the end of the book, Liv is convinced the sheriff wants the Makers' help patrolling the neighborhood. Do you agree with her? Why or why not?

GRAB YOUR MAKER NOTEBOOK!

1. Compare and contrast yourself with one of the Mysterious Makers. How are you alike? How are you different?

2. Pick a scene in which you disagreed with how a character handled a situation. Rewrite it in the way you think it should have happened.

3. Think about the scene where the thief is scared by Liv. Try rewriting it from the thief's perspective. What is he thinking? How is he feeling?

THE FUN DOESN'T STOP HERE:

Discover more at www.capstonekids.com

- Videos & Contests
- Games & Puzzles
- Friends & Favorites
- Authors & Illustrators

Find cool websites and more books like this one at www.facthound.com. Just type in the Book ID: 9781496546760 and you're ready to go!

READ MORE MAKERS ADVENTURES!

Bake And Be Blessed

Bread baking as a metaphor for spiritual growth

this book has been
Donated

in
Loving
Memory
of

Candace Lyn Johnson

Father Dominic Garramone, OSB

Dedication

This book is dedicated
to all those who have baked and broken bread
at the Crumpled House

Deo Optimo Maximo

Introduction

In the summer of 1986, I attended an institute for junior Benedictine monks at Holy Cross Abbey in Canon City, Colorado. The institute brought young monks together for studies with scholars from various abbeys and to strengthen the bonds of fellowship throughout the order. We had classes in the morning, work assignments in the afternoon, and took part in the life and prayer of the local community. Incidentally, the week we arrived, the abbey's baker got the flu, and I was given the run of the kitchen in the evening, earning me the nickname "Dominic Vosbiscuits" (a play on words from the Latin "Dominus vosbicsum"—"The Lord be with you").

One of our classes was a study of the scriptural references in the Rule of Saint Benedict, under the direction of Abbot Martin Burne, OSB. There are about 250 direct quotations or allusions to Sacred Scripture in the Rule, and Abbot Martin would assign one or two to each participant every day. We were expected to offer the class a brief commentary on our assigned passage and how it relates to everyday life in the monastery. One of the first passages I received was from the chapter on the qualities of the abbot: "Everything he teaches and commands should, like the leaven of divine justice, permeate the minds of his disciples" (RB 2:5). The allusion here is to the parable of the yeast in Matthew 13:33, where the kingdom of God is compared to the yeast a woman kneads into the dough until the whole batch is leavened.

For my commentary I compared the abbot to a baker, who has to build character in the community in much the same way a baker develops character in dough. He must ensure that the community has balance and proportion, like the ingredients in a recipe, and must "stir things up" to keep the monks from becoming complacent. The abbot must "knead" the community through the daily disciplines of prayer and silence, and give them periods of rest, like the dough rising under a towel in a warm place. Sometimes, the community has to be "punched down" for the sake of humility, and it is shaped by obedience into loaves. Finally, I said, the abbot must test the community in the fires of self-sacrifice, to prepare them to be broken and shared with the hungry.

Having just baked bread the night before, it hadn't taken much effort for me to come up with this interpretation, and I didn't expect much of a reaction. After all, what could be more ordinary than bread? But Abbot Martin thanked me for an excellent presentation and suggested that I write an article on the subject for the *American Benedictine Review*.

At the time I didn't think that a monk in the second year of simple vows should be telling abbots how to do their job, so that article was never written. But in the very real sense, preparation for this book began at that institute.

Since then, I have taken solemn vows as a monk, earned two master's degrees, been ordained as a priest, and taped three seasons of the public television baking show *Breaking Bread With Father Dominic*. But none of these achievements really prepared me to write this book; rather, it was *living* the daily life in community. I'm not suggesting that my time in seminary was wasted: I had excellent teachers who gave me a first-rate pastoral and theological education, especially in liturgy and Sacred Scripture. But reading about Jesus washing the feet of his disciples took on its full meaning only when I was assigned to give an elderly brother his daily bath. Studying the history behind the rubrics for the rituals of the Mass was easy compared to learning how to celebrate daily Eucharist in a way that makes the Living Christ present to *this* community, right *now*, in *this* place. In the last analysis, "head knowledge" is a support for Christian living, not a substitute.

You do not need a master's degree in theological studies in order to grow spiritually. The life you are living *right now* is preparing you to be a deeply spiritual person, if you are intentional about how you live. What is required is "sacramental awareness"—a kind of vision that allows one to perceive God's presence and action in ordinary things. In the sacrament of baptism, God uses the physical, earthly element of water to symbolize the forgiveness of sin and the spiritual rebirth of the baptized person. Sacramental awareness is based on the belief that God uses the stuff of this life to reveal the divine saving love and grace, not only in the official sacraments of the church, but in everyday life as well. Joseph Crockett describes how one develops this awareness in *Teaching Scripture From an African-American Perspective:*

> The sanctuary strategy of education is grounded in the understanding that God is ever-present and that God's omnipresence makes possible the transformation of every ordinary place into a sacred place. When persons recognize and respond obediently to God's presence, transformation from the ordinary to the sacred takes place and sanctuary is experienced.[1]

To some, it may seem novel to consider the home as a sanctuary, a sacred place where one encounters God's presence and power, but in fact this concept has been a part of monastic tradition for centuries. St. Benedict refers to the monastery as "a school for the Lord's service" (RB Prol. 45) and created regulations for every aspect of the monks' lives: working, eating, sleeping, praying, reading, etc. But he didn't create laws for their own sake, but to remind the monks that every activity of every minute of the day is an opportunity to encounter God. For example, St. Benedict writes that the tools of the monastery should be regarded as the sacred

---

1 Joseph V. Crockett, *Teaching Scripture From an African American Perspective* (Discipleship Resources, Nashville, TN) p. 28.

vessels of the altar (RB 31:10) and therefore treated with the same reverence. In that way, daily labor can be seen as contributing to the sanctification of the individual and that of the community as well. In the Benedictine view, every activity can teach us something about our relationship with God.

This book is about what one specific activity, baking bread, can teach us about growing spiritually. I have neither the education nor the wisdom to describe every aspect of the spiritual life, so I won't attempt it here. But I have baked a lot of bread in my life, and done a lot of thinking and praying in the process, trying to develop my own sacramental awareness of God's presence and action. I have been surprised by the divine lessons found in what for me are ordinary activities: measuring ingredients, mixing, kneading, shaping dough, baking and breaking bread.

You don't have to be an experienced baker to understand the reflections in this book, although many of the images will resonate more deeply if you have spent some time with your hands on a batch of bread dough. I'll begin with an explanation on how bread baking itself can be a spiritual experience that reintegrates our mind, body and soul when we've been fragmented by a too-busy schedule. A kind of baker's checklist follows in the next chapter, so you can find out if you have all the ingredients necessary for your recipe for spiritual growth. Chapter three offers a reflection on grinding grain as analogous to intercessory prayer, while chapter four explores the idea of yeast as a symbol for the gospel principles that should enliven our Christian vocation. In chapter five, we'll see how mixing and kneading the dough is a metaphor for daily meditation, and I'll describe a traditional method for reading sacred scripture in a prayerful way. Since the dough has to rest in order to rise, in chapter six we'll explore the importance of rest and relaxation in the spiritual life. I'll recount two stories of being "punched down" in chapter seven–I'm sure you'll be able to relate to the feeling–and suggest how we can grow from such experiences. Chapter eight describes how we are transformed by the fires of suffering, just as dough is transformed in the heat of oven into bread. We'll see that Christian service means to be broken and shared with others in chapter nine, and find out why it's essential first to be blessed. In chapter ten we'll try to develop an appreciation for crusts and crumbs and understand why Jesus values them. In chapter eleven, I'll offer some initial reflections on the question, "What kind of bread shall we be?" and in chapter twelve share some insights I've received from others on that same question since the publication of the first edition.

Each chapter will include some information about the hows and whys of bread baking and this new edition has a few more recipes than the previous one, which I hope will delight the hard core Breadheads of the world. But in this book, the meaning of baking is more important than the method, and the recipes are more of a bonus than a focus. Although I've produced four cookbooks and have a fourth in the works, I've maintained all along that people don't need recipes, they need reasons to bake. You can find hundreds of recipes at your local library, tens of thousands of them if you have access to the Internet. But all the best recipes in culinary history won't make you bake bread unless it feeds your spirit as well as your body. I hope this book will give you reasons to "bake and be blessed."

Since I often write about my mother, I thought you might want to know what she looks like all dressed up… and what she's like on the inside! As far back as I can remember, she's always looked for reasons to bake, even something as simple as melted ice cream. This first recipe uses only two ingredients—melted ice cream and self-rising flour—to make muffins. The results are so surprisingly good, you'll be tempted to leave ice cream out on the counter on purpose! Premium ice creams will produce a richer muffins with more tender crumb.

One of my favorite memories of this recipe is from a "bread retreat" I gave at the Franciscan Center in Tampa, Florida. After everyone had arrived and signed in, we took several flavors of ice cream out of the freezer to thaw. Then we went to the chapel for the opening conference and evening prayer. By then the ice cream was soupy and warm, ready to mix with the self-rising flour to make a late snack for the group. We stood around in the kitchen, laughing and sharing, getting to know each other as we broke bread together.

Ice Cream Muffins

Yield: 6 muffins

1 cup self-rising flour (see note)
1 to 1 ½ cups melted ice cream, any flavor

Put flour in medium bowl. Stir in enough of the melted ice cream to make a thick batter. If the ice cream has chocolate-chips or nuts, make sure they get mixed in, too. (You can also add nuts or candy to the mix, as desired.)

Lightly grease a 6-cup muffin tin. Divide batter among muffin cups. Bake in a preheated 375-degree oven 12 to 15 minutes, or until a toothpick inserted into the center of a muffin comes out clean. The tops of the muffins will not brown very much, but will spring back when lightly pressed.

Let muffins cool to lukewarm, then eat immediately. Feel free to dunk pieces of the muffin in any remaining melted ice cream.

Note: If you don't have self-rising flour on hand, you can substitute 1 cup all-purpose flour plus 1 ½ teaspoons baking powder and ⅛ teaspoon salt.

Chapter One
Bread Baking As Spiritual Exercise

The main thrust of this book is how bread baking is a *metaphor* for spiritual growth, but the very act of mixing, kneading, shaping and baking a loaf of homemade bread is *itself* a spiritual act, one which nourishes us on a variety of levels. Before we examine the symbolic value of these activities, let's look at how bread baking can directly feed the mind and the spirit as well as the body. It's a lesson I learned not in the monastery, but in my mother's kitchen.

I was blessed to grow up in a baking home. My mom baked bread and cookies for as long as I can remember, as did my Grandma Tootsie, who lived with us after Grandpa Frankie died. We kids were always in the kitchen with them, and I can honestly say I don't recall either of them ever saying "Get out of my way!" Instead, we heard things like, "Here, beat these eggs for me," or "Reach into that bottom cabinet and get out the mixer," and, of course, "Who wants to lick the spoon?"

My mother used the kitchen much like a practical one-room schoolhouse. The kitchen was where we learned our numbers: "I need six cups of flour," she'd say. "Who's going to count for me?" We'd all raise our hands like kindergartners: "Ooh! Ooh! Pick me!" Or we'd have to count Hershey's Kisses as we unwrapped them for peanut blossoms, or the number of slices in a loaf of bread. Other recipes gave us the opportunity to work on fractions: "These cookies call for three-quarters of a cup of sugar, but we're making a double batch—how much flour do we need?" (To this day I can scale just about any recipe in my head.) Learning to tell time was also accomplished in the kitchen: "This bread bakes for 45 minutes—what time will it be when it comes out?" With my mom, every recipe was an opportunity for learning.

My experience of bread baking, however, began as a class project in the fifth grade, at Sacred Heart School in Peoria, Illinois. The school had an accelerated curriculum, which included French class from fourth grade onward. One day our teacher, Mrs. Elson, gave an assignment to bring to class an ethnic food from a French-speaking country, and each student was scheduled to bring a dish on a different day. So I went home and said those words that every mother dreads to hear: "Mom, we have to do a class project."

Fortunately, I was the third of five children, so the prospect of "food homework" didn't faze my mother at all. Mama Garramone answered without hesitation: "Let's make French bread—that's easy." Anyone who has had a yeast bread disaster in the kitchen might have suggested French toast made with Wonder bread, but Mom had won dozens of ribbons at the Heart of Illinois Fair for her baking. So the day before it was my turn to play a pint-sized French chef in class, she taught me how to make French baguettes.

The details of that first baking lesson are lost to conscious memory, or have been blended with a thousand other occasions of my mother's gentle instruction as a baker. Surprisingly, I don't recall what the loaves looked like either, and if a photo was taken, it's lost or buried. I do know that I took the baguettes to school with a cutting board, my mom's best bread knife (with dire consequences if I failed to return with it), a pound of unsalted butter, and a jar of homemade apricot preserves. What I remember most of all was the appearance of my project *after* my presentation: a cutting board littered with crumbs, a martyred tub of butter, and an empty jar with jam running down the sides and the sticky spoon still in it. And I recall with startling clarity how that sight made me feel: *Wow. I baked bread, and they really* liked *it. I did OK.*

Although I wouldn't recognize it until years later, this was my first hint that bread baking itself is a spiritual experience. I don't mean to suggest that it was a particularly *religious* experience—I doubt we said grace before cutting into the loaves, nor at the moment did I intuit any connection between baguettes and the Lord's Supper. But baking bread and seeing my classmates (with an exuberance that only children can bring to the table) devour it eagerly had somehow nourished my spirit as well. The desire for affirmation, fellowship, accomplishment, recognition—those interior hungers that can be as painfully acute in children as in adults—all were fed in the act of breaking bread with others.

Since then I've discovered that bread baking is a unifying activity, one that can re-integrate our fragmented selves. Life pulls us in many directions, between work and home, obligations to the community and our responsibilities for our families. The result can be a vague feeling of incompleteness, which is well described by Henri Nouwen:

> The great paradox of our time is that many of us are busy and bored at the same time. While running from one event to the next, we wonder in our innermost selves if anything is really happening. While we can hardly keep up with our many tasks and obligations, we are not so sure that it would make any difference if we did nothing at all. While people keep pushing us in all directions, we doubt if anyone really cares. In short, while our lives are full, we feel unfulfilled.[1]

Bread baking is a not cure for all of modern society's ills, but it can be a means by which, on a given day, we reintegrate our fragmented selves by engaging mind, body, emotions and spirit in an intentional act of creativity.

---

1 Henri J. M. Nouwen, Making All Things New (Harper and Row, NY 1981) p. 30.

By baking bread we can reel in our distracted minds by concentrating on the details of the recipe. We must gather ingredients, understand the logical sequence of instructions, concern ourselves with measurement, time and temperature. It's an orderly process when so much of life is random, even chaotic. Sometimes when I have the greatest number of things to do, like during production week of the school musical, I make time to bake bread to reorder my mental faculties.

Distraction during the process of mixing can lead to disaster. Once I made what appeared to be the most exquisite cornmeal muffins of my entire baking career. Each one was perfectly formed, identical in size and shape, and baked to the ideal golden color—the pinnacle of muffinhood. Alas, I was not paying very close attention during the mixing process, as I discovered when I broke one open, still slightly steaming from the oven, and popped a piece in my mouth. It was like taking a bite out of a salt block—I had evidently measured out a quarter cup of salt instead of the sugar that was called for in the recipe! The next batch tasted better (I'm glad I did a taste test instead of simply serving them to the brethren!) but I have never since made muffins that looked so beautiful.

Baking is also a mental exercise because there is so much to learn about the way dough is formed: how water interacts with flour, what yeast does for the recipe and why kneading gives the dough its lively character. (Don't worry, I'll address all these questions later on—stay with me.) Sometimes we learn the hard way. When I first experimented with pumpernickel bread, my earliest attempts were unbelievably heavy. One loaf was so dense that when sliced it produced no crumbs—fragments kept getting sucked back into its gravity field. But I had never even eaten pumpernickel, let alone baked it, so in my ignorance I put one of these leaden loaves out on the monastery lunch table. Later that day I asked Fr. James what he thought of it. He paused, (searching, I suspect, for a gentle way of saying that it was loathsome) and then said tentatively, "It needs more . . . air . . . in it . . . somehow." I discovered I had a lot to learn about how to get more "air" into heavy breads like rye and pumpernickel. Even failures in baking can lead us to sharpen our wits on the whetstone of experience, and study what went wrong and why.[2]

A few years ago I received an e-mail that showed me that even watching someone bake or cook can have a powerful effect on the memory and the emotions. It came from a viewer who had suffered a car accident that caused considerable physical damage, and which also affected her brain, causing her to lose portions of her memory. On one particularly discouraging day, her husband thought to administer a little extra love and attention. I'll let her letter (used with permission) tell the rest of the story:

> My husband sat me down in front of the television....brought my ice packs, a cup of coffee and a cookie... and he flipped channels. I saw Narsi David on channel 9... I asked to watch it. I remembered when I had met Narsi at the Gilroy Garlic Festival so many years before. Then... Martin Yan who I had met also... I started remembering!!!
>
> So I watched... and watched... show after show... and memories came back into my hurt brain... family events and outings... people I knew all associated with FOOD... (I'm Italian... that should explain why I associate food with all that!!) I remembered as a little girl watching the Galloping Gourmet and Julia Child with my Grandma!!!
>
> The day went by... I was more comfortable. I actually relaxed. And I think that it was the first day I remembered how to feel happy!
>
> Between shows... I took a break and I also took a

2 One of the best books for this purpose is Shirley Corriher's *Cookwise*, in which she illuminates the invisible processes of all sorts of cooking and baking, including from simple omelets to French pastry. Shirley is one of hundreds of excellent teachers who can both engage your mind and expand it, and they're no farther than the nearest bookstore or library.

minute to pray. I thanked God for these pleasures and for the happiness that I felt in my heart from all of this. How I felt refreshed and had learned that cooking and food was something that I could still do. And how it connected me with the world and my life... before the accident... and now!

The next show on was yours! I had never seen it before...! You were telling me all about how I should not be afraid to try new things... don't worry if it doesn't look the way you expect or want it to be... take your time and feel how it all comes together... effort makes a good end result... WOW!!!

Today... I still have much to do... doctors, surgeries and procedures, physical therapy... but I have goals, and dreams of what I can do. My mandatory periods of rest are no longer unwelcome on Saturday mornings, as I look forward to watching and learning more from the beautiful shows.
And best of all, I have fresh baked bread!!

Thank you & God Bless!
Rhonda

If my show got had had gotten terrible ratings and folded after a single season, it would have been worth it for the sake of this one woman.

Bread baking helps us focus our minds, but it also gives our bodies a workout—it's a spiritual exercise precisely because it *is* exercise. The purely *physical* effort of mixing and kneading can be one of its chief benefits, by which vigorous effort can alleviate a boring day of crunching numbers. Kneading is a stress-reliever *par excellence*, a mindless, repetitive, almost violent motion, like a long run or laps in the pool. However, I take issue with people who say kneading is good therapy, as if you have to be dysfunctional in order to enjoy its benefits. I prefer to think of baking as preventative medicine, which keeps you from needing therapy in the first place.

One can also appreciate the way baking reclaims our physical selves from fragmentation by involving all of the senses during the baking process. The ultimate goal is the taste of the bread, but along the way one gets to enjoy the smell of the yeast and the texture of the dough, the scent of herbs and their wildly different shades of green. The sensual pleasure of baking includes the smooth surface of an egg and the gritty grain of salt and sugar. It's the glorious sight of a shiny brown crust of whole wheat bread, and the crackly sound of the perfect pizza crust as you roll the cutter through the cheese and toppings to make wedges or squares. It's the way the house smells when you make cranberry orange bran muffins, and the way the whole block smells when you bake garlic bread. It's the feel of a soft, warm bun as you hold it in your hand to butter it, and the texture of a crusty roll against your teeth as you bite through to the fluffy interior. Don't tell me that bread machine bread is as good as a loaf made from scratch. Its convenience comes at too steep a price. I prefer not to impoverish my senses to amass a wealth of time.

There is yet one other way in which the body is affected spiritually by baking bread: we are forced to slow down and stay put. The dough is like a baby—it may nap for a while, but we dare not leave it alone too long. Bread baking makes us stay put and let ourselves be found in the same place for a couple of hours, to be in a still and stable place in a whirling world. My friend Mary has been baking a lot more since she got my cookbooks. She wrote and told me that her family has gotten used to her being around the house more while she bakes. One afternoon she had a batch of dough rising and had just punched it down when her teenage son Michael came into the kitchen. He started sharing with her about his hopes and dreams for the future—like most teens, something he rarely does. She left the dough on the counter (she knew it would forgive her!), and just sat and listened, grateful that by taking time for the bread, she had taken time for her son as well.

Clearly, bread baking can benefit our emotions, which are closely allied to our spiritual selves. Bread baking is like aromatherapy—but better, since you can't eat a lighted candle. The scent of fresh bread can evoke feelings of comfort, nostalgia and love, and does wonders for our spirit before we even take a bite. When I'm sad or depressed (yes, it even happens to monks!), the smell of homemade bread can do wonders for my mental health.

The recipe itself can form an emotional bond with a loved one. It might be Grandma's refrigerator rolls that she made every time you spent the weekend there, or mom's *povitica* that she made only at Christmas and Easter, so you do the same. It may be that the recipe came from a cookbook received as an especially thoughtful gift, or found by accident in a tiny bookstore you stepped into to get out of the rain. For many people, bread recipes are an integral part of their cultural heritage, perhaps lost for awhile and only now being rediscovered. The spirit of our ancestors lives on in our hands as we knead the dough, shaping loaves as they have been shaped for centuries.

Often the act of baking is charged with meaning because of the utensils you use. Most bakers have a favorite bowl: a wedding gift, an antique mall treasure, one with no particular history except that it has steeper sides to keep the flour under control. Spoons, measuring cups, rolling pins, even dish towels might be associated with a dear friend or relative, making the act of baking a way to connect with them.

Even when I'm alone in the abbey kitchen, baking is a family affair. Recently I baked an accordion bread, with dough folded back and forth between layers of sun dried tomatoes, green onions and Romano cheese. I got the recipe from my sister Angela, mixed the ingredients with a dough whisk my mother found at a rummage sale, in a stoneware bowl my brother Marty had a family friend make. I used a flour sifter from my sister Eileen, rolled the dough out with a hardwood rolling pin my father turned on his lathe, and baked it on a pizza stone that was a birthday present from one of my students. Alone in the kitchen? Not in my house!

Small things, you might say, but that is precisely where sacramental awareness has the power to give greater meaning to our lives. Few if any of us receive awesome theophanies in which God reveals the divine presence in all its majesty. In Exodus 33:18-23 Moses asks to see God's glory. The Lord replies that Moses would not be able to bear it, and instead tells him, "When my glory passes I will set you in the hollow of the rock and cover you with my hand until I have passed by. Then I shall remove my hand, so that you may see my back, but my face is not to be seen." One preacher put it this way: "Sometimes the Lord's backside is the only view that's available!" Seen in a more positive light, sacramental awareness helps us catch glimpses of God, like finding footprints and fingerprints that remind us that God has been around and is up to something. The small blessings of family and fellowship are God's everyday means of loving us. It is the daily dew and the light afternoon shower that keeps the garden of our souls growing, rather than a once-a-year downpour of grace.

All the processes that I have described as reintegrating our mind, body and emotions also feed the spirit. Even as I'm using my mind to read instructions and measure ingredients, I'm also recalling passages from Sacred Scripture associated with baking: the unleavened bread of Passover, the manna in the wilderness, and the showbread of the daily temple offering; Paul's exhortation to the Corinthians to beware the yeast of malice and wickedness; Jesus' parable of the yeast, the multiplication of the loaves, even the wheat and the weeds, and of course, the Bread of Life, the Eucharist, the *panis angelicus*.

I'm not saying that all these passages come crowding between the ingredients every time I bake. But living in the monastery, steeped in Scripture hour by hour and year by year, I find that verses rise up like bubbles in a sourdough sponge and burst into consciousness at unexpected times. The mind and the memory are linked to spiritual realities.

So is the body. When we reclaim our fragmented physical selves and appreciate the "bodily"-ness of bread baking, our spirit has to come along—it gets hijacked on the sensory joyride. Those who have experienced the quiet joys of baking can attest to the wonders of feeling a lump of dough come to life beneath their hands. Like the gardener who sifts the soil between outstretched, reverent fingers, or the potter who caresses the whirling clay, the baker can feel that wordless, mystical bond between creator and creation. Baking also engages our spiritual side by requiring us to be patient with the process (and with ourselves), to slow down and respect the limitations imposed by an intentional act of artistic expression. Stop and smell the roses? Better still to stop and smell the rosemary basil focaccia that is just now emerging from the oven.

But even apart from the sensual delights of mixing, kneading and baking bread, the act of eating is itself a spiritual act, or more accurately, dining, feasting, *breaking bread together* is a sacred, joyful, spiritual experience. Baking invites and creates community. Although most of us could eat an entire loaf of bread straight from the oven by ourselves, most often bakers are eager to share. The very word "companion" comes from the Latin *cum pane*: "with bread." A companion is someone with whom we share our bread, and we bake a special loaf when company is coming. I'm sometimes distressed when someone says, "I used to bake bread all the time when my children were younger, but now that it's just me and my husband…" I always say, "God bless you, but don't you have any neighbors?"

Ultimately for Christians, baking bread is a spiritual experience because Jesus made food and fellowship the core of his ministry. His first miracle was at a wedding party; his biggest miracle was a picnic for 5,000; his last meal was his most important lesson. "Take this bread and eat," he said, "for this is my body." Take and eat, take and drink, do this, remember this, BE THIS, in memory of Me. Be the bread for the world, be shaped by experience, by the neediness of the people around you and the people half a world away. Rest in a warm place when you need to, but be prepared for the world to punch you down. Be transformed in the fires of suffering, be blessed, be broken, be shared.

Christ calls us to live in imitation of him, the Bread of Life. If we are serious about living a more meaningful life, we have to assemble all the important "ingredients" for spiritual growth. In the next chapter, we'll look at what's necessary to accomplish that task, what chefs call the *"mise en place."*

Chapter Two
Mise En Place

When I was preparing to tape an episode of *Breaking Bread*, I had to make a daily list of instructions for my kitchen crew. This list, usually written in marker on a large flip chart, included a schedule for what needed to be prepared for use on camera, whether it's utensils, a set of ingredients, risen dough or a finished loaf. Our nickname for a complete set of pre-measured ingredients in bowls is an "A-14." When we started taping the first season, I made the list on a legal pad, and abbreviated "Assemble Ingredients For" as "A-I-4," as in "A-I-4 Butter Pecan Breakfast Bread." But my letter "I" was mistaken for the number "1" and "A-14" became our official shorthand.

Bread baking for TV presents unique difficulties, distinct from other cooking shows. Because the process of raising dough is relatively slow (compared, say, to peeling potatoes or trimming fat off a steak), we have to be well-organized to keep a reasonable shooting schedule and produce a program of consistent quality. Stopping in the middle of a take because we've forgotten an ingredient or utensil is costly and annoying.

So to get good results in baking, even at home, you have to be prepared. That may seem pretty obvious, but often we fail to apply this simple principle to our spiritual life. Rather than have a plan or a program for our spiritual growth, we simply let things happen: praying when we feel like it; perhaps attending Mass or church services regularly, perhaps not;

occasionally picking up a book on prayer or a commentary on Scripture if we happen to see one or receive it as a gift. We may make a greater effort to plan at certain times of year (e.g., Lent or Advent), but both our planning and our subsequent efforts are often halfhearted at best.

The need to be intentional about our spiritual growth is illustrated by the insight of a college student who attended an evening workshop on prayer that I organized at a parish in Louisville, Kentucky. I asked the participants, all single adult Catholics, to compare their prayer life to their eating habits. "If you were to eat only as often as you pray," I asked, "what would your 'diet' be like?" A number of people had some excellent analogies, saying that they gorge themselves on Sunday and starve the rest of the week, or that they "snack" on prayer all day but once a day they have to make time for a full meal. One young man had the most honest response: "If prayer is like food, then I feel like I'm unconscious and being fed intravenously. I need to wake up and eat for myself."

What can bread baking teach us about organizing our lives to progress in faith? What we need in our spiritual life is what professional chefs call the *mise en place* (French for "put in place"). Just as my staff does for the pre-production "A-14," we all need to assemble the utensils and ingredients necessary for our recipe for spiritual growth. Usually head chefs hand this task over to an underling, but since we're going to "cook" for ourselves, we need some guidelines for gathering the materials and resources necessary to sustain our growth in holiness. What follows is a series of questions to explore as we begin this task.

1. Do you have a recipe for spiritual growth, that is, an actual plan or routine?

An experienced baker can improvise and successfully create delicious breads without a recipe, but only after years of trial and error, learning from both success and failure. Most of us need a list of ingredients and some general instructions in order to produce a credible loaf, and the same is true of prayer. In the spiritual life, it's a rare person who can advance in holiness without an intentional plan or routine.

Admittedly this is easier in a monastery where several times a day a bell rings to summon the community to spiritual exercises, and no one is expected to be doing anything else. But even monks need to reserve time for private prayer and spiritual reflection. In my Benedictine community of Saint Bede, monks are expected to spend about an hour a day in personal spiritual exercises, and each monk chooses that time according to his own schedule. Anyone who is serious about spiritual growth has to make time every day for prayer, reading and reflection.

Many people may respond to the previous statement: "I don't have time." I can relate. Not long ago the prior asked me to take one of the older monks to a morning doctor's appointment an hour and a half away. By the time I returned it was mid-afternoon. Then Br. Bede called to ask me to fix supper for the community since our regular cook had called in sick. I had to miss evening prayer because I was busy preparing beef tips over noodles (which, incidentally, fused into a solid mass upon their removal from the giant steam boiler). The peas were frozen, and I started them so late that they never did make it to the table. After this less-than-TV-perfect supper, I cleaned the kitchen just in time to go to Compline, the last prayer of the day. As I slumped in my choir stall, I thought of how nice it was going to be to relax for the rest of the evening, only to realize that the stage crew was scheduled to come out at 8 o'clock that night. My first thought is not fit to print, but my second thought was a true revelation: *I wonder if this is what it feels like to be a single mom?* God bless you if you are one of those people who live that life every day.

Nonetheless, I want to challenge people who say they have no time to ask themselves this question: "If spiritual growth is truly important to me, what changes would I need to make in my life in order to create time and space for personal prayer?"

Sometimes people are hesitant to answer that question because they feel guilty for taking time for themselves. After all, if I'm spending time on *me*, I'm *not* spending it on someone else, right?

In answer I offer an insight from my college Greek teacher, Dr. Marietta Conroy. She taught New Testament Greek to college seminarians, but also offered insights into the spiritual life that have stayed with me over the years. Once we were translating Matthew 11:28: "Come to me, all you who are weary and are burdened, and I will give you rest." After we had discussed the grammatical points of the text, she put her book down and looked at us intently. "I want you to remember when you are priests, gentlemen," she intoned, "that if you do too many things out of the goodness of your heart, eventually the heart ceases to be good."

Dr. Conroy's comment holds equally true for all Christians. We all need to recharge our spiritual reserves, and if we fail to do so, we lose the very qualities we are trying hardest to cultivate. If I don't spend time in personal prayer and meditation on the Scriptures, I won't have anything to say in the pulpit. We can't share the Good News with others unless we're faithfully pursuing our own journey in daily prayer and meditation. The old Latin aphorism is *Nemo dat quod non habet*: You can't give what you ain't got!

In addition to making time for spiritual exercises, it also helps to have a goal. It might be to read a chapter of the Bible a day, or to finish all the works of Thomas Merton or C.S. Lewis. One might choose to explore a theological discipline, like contemporary moral issues or the Incarnation. Learning about other faiths and reading their sacred writings could become an important goal for spiritual growth.

It is important that such a goal be measurable and realistic. To be measurable it should be possible to perceive when the goal is met. For example, if our goal is something vague like "to be more patient," then we never meet the goal, because we can always be more patient than we are now. But if you set the more specific goal "I will read what the writings of St. Paul say about patience and find alternatives to yelling when I need to correct my children," then you can actually measure your progress. You can gauge how much you've read and prayed, and if you have indeed discovered new ways to express love through Christian discipline.

A goal must also be realistic. At a Speaking of Women's Health Conference in St. Louis, I suggested a variety of spiritual goals concerned with relationships: to find ways to defuse gossip at the workplace, to learn to say "I love you" more often to one's parents, etc. When I got to "forgive your ex-husband," one woman called out, "That's gonna take a few years, Father!" We all laughed, and I agreed that "realistic" doesn't always mean "short term." But I also reminded her that if she doesn't set the goal and take steps to achieve it, it won't happen.

2. Do you have the right utensils and ingredients?

Just like a baker must check her pantry to see if she has enough flour and the right size bowl, we need to be sure that we have the necessary resources to support our spiritual endeavors. Don't panic–just like bread baking, it can be done with a few simple tools and ingredients. Daily prayer and meditation require very little to be successful. Viewers of *Breaking Bread* know that I like gadgets (the non-electric kind), but when it comes to prayer, it's best to keep things simple. Here are the essentials:

- **A quiet place where you can be undisturbed.** This "ingredient" is often the hardest to locate, but unless you have astonishing powers of concentration even in the midst of chaos, silence and solitude are substantial elements for developing a meaningful prayer life. Sometimes this requires real creativity, especially if you have children in the house. When my sister Angela, the eldest of the family, was a toddler, my mother discovered an inventive way to get her to take a nap in the summertime. Every afternoon, the ice cream truck drove through our neighborhood playing that unmistakable tinkling music. The first time my sister heard it, she asked my mother, "What is that sound?" My mother replied, "That's the angels playing the music that says it's time for little girls and boys to take a nap." My sister went to her bedroom without argument, every time.

- A **comfortable place to sit.** Almost everyone has a favorite chair that fits one's contours perfectly. Your favorite chair may not be the best possible place to pray if it's so comfortable that it induces sleep! I can't pray in a recliner or on a sofa, even sitting up straight, because all the cushions tempt me to nap. I much prefer to pray in my rocking chair in my room, or in one of the patio chairs by the pond in the west garden of the abbey. Both are comfortable but not overly soft. For several years I prayed sitting cross-legged on a Zen meditation pillow, and our Fr. James keeps a kneeler in his room for prayer. You'll have to choose for yourself.

- **A recent translation of the Bible.** The Bible is the prayer book par excellence, and it's worth the investment to buy a good one in hardback. Which translation you use is a matter of personal preference, but initially it's best to use the same one that is used at your church. That way when you attend church services, the readings will resonate more deeply with your own meditations and make the experience more meaningful. As you grow more confident you might try different translations—rather like trying a new bread recipe or adding different grains to a familiar loaf—to see what new ideas arise from a text with a new flavor. If you can read in a foreign language, all the better. Some people like a Bible with commentary or notes explaining difficult parts of the text, but be careful not to let Bible-based prayer turn into mere study.

The three elements mentioned above are all that's absolutely necessary for beginning to grow spiritually through prayer and meditation, but here are some other possible aids to prayer:

- A journal or notebook for written reflection
- A crucifix, cross or other religious image on which to focus during prayer
- Instrumental music to help you relax
- Candles or incense to create a sacred space
- Other inspirational reading materials.

We'll revisit these tools for prayer in more detail in the chapter "Mixing, Kneading and Meditation," and offer more specific methods for prayer.

3. Is the oven hot? What part of the day is your high energy time? Your low point? Do the activities at those times match your energy level? When is your usual prayer time?

I have never been much of a morning person, and the fact that I have been called to become a monk with prayers at 6:00 a.m. makes me wonder about God's sense of humor sometimes! Since my undergraduate degree is in theater, I developed an internal clock by which my high energy time is from 8:00 p.m. until midnight. That's when I can be my most creative, alert and enthusiastic (much of this book was written well after sunset). So if I want my prayer life to be dynamic and imaginative, I have to schedule time for meditation in the evening. If I want my prayer to be more relaxed and reflective, I'll take time in the late afternoon. But if I try to do private prayer in the morning, I'm drowsy and lethargic.

We all have our own internal energy cycle, dictating when the most productive times of day occur. If we are serious about our recipe for spiritual growth, then we have to choose a time when the oven is hot, that is, when we have the emotional and mental energy for sustained, deliberate concentration. I am referring here to the time for a prolonged period of prayer, thirty minutes or more. We may engage in briefer periods of prayer throughout the day, but a more extensive daily exercise is also recommended.

I once shared my discoveries about prayer times at a workshop for deacons and their wives. After my conference, one woman came up to me and thanked me for telling her it was OK to pray according to her own schedule. "I'd always read that you were supposed to pray in the morning," she said sheepishly, "and I always doze off! But when I pray in the afternoon, I get so much more out of it." We agreed that one should at least make a morning offering or spend a short time in prayer at the beginning of the day, but that for us, the better time for prayer was later.

If you discover at the end of the day that you haven't yet had time for prayer, you can at least practice a traditional spiritual exercise known as the examen (pronounced ex-AY-men). In examen, we review the events of the day by looking at our actions and attitudes from morning to night in order to perceive how God has been at work. Remember that business about God's footprints and fingerprints from the last chapter? Examen helps us sharpen our sacramental awareness. We might do an examination of conscience in order to recognize and acknowledge our sinfulness, but the focus should be on God's presence and action throughout the day. We might be surprised to see how God has been guiding us, speaking to us through people and events, showing His love in ways that were hidden to us by the stresses of the day. Regular practice of the examen eventually makes us more tuned to the divine presence in everyday life.

One of the best books about examen is *Sleeping With Bread: Holding On to What Gives You Life*.[1] The authors tell the story of how children who had been moved to safety in refugee camps during World War II often had trouble getting to sleep. Someone had the inspiration to give each child a piece of bread before bed, which they could eat right then or

---

1 By Dennis Linn, Sheila Fabricant Linn and Matthew Linn (Paulist Press, June 1995).

save until the next day. Thus the children were reassured that just as they had been fed and cared for today, the same would be true tomorrow. The authors suggest that doing an examen before bed has a similar effect: We can see that God has cared for us on this day, and can have faith that He will do the same tomorrow.

Since the purpose of a mise en place is to make sure you have every ingredient, I thought I'd share a recipe I created with lots of them–fifteen, if you count the salsa and guacamole at the end. "Inside Out Nacho Bread" has all the goodies that go on top of nachos, inside a sour cream-based cornbread. Believe me, if you like loaded nachos, the results will be entirely worth it.

I think I'm missing something, but I'm not sure what it is...

Inside Out Nacho Bread

¼ cup (half a stick) butter, chilled, + 1 tablespoon
1 cup chopped onion
1 ¼ cups yellow cornmeal
1 cup all-purpose flour
¼ cup sugar
1 tablespoon baking powder
1 ½ teaspoons salt
½ teaspoon baking soda
3 eggs, well beaten
1 ½ cups sour cream
1 ½ cups shredded cheddar cheese
1/3 cup chopped black olives
¼ cup minced jalapeno peppers

Over medium heat, sauté the onion in 1 tablespoon of butter until tender, about 10 minutes. Set aside to cool. Sift cornmeal, flour, sugar, baking powder, salt and baking soda into a medium size bowl and stir to blend. Cut the butter into the dry ingredients using a pastry cutter or two knives until the mixture resembles coarse crumbs. Add sour cream and eggs and stir until blended. Mix in the cheese, olives, and peppers. Pour the batter into a greased 11 inch stoneware deep dish pizza pan, or a 9 x 9 x 2-inch cake pan. Bake in a preheated 400 degree oven for 35 to 40 minutes, or until golden brown and a cake tester inserted into the center comes out clean. Cool for 15 to 20 minutes in the pan before cutting into wedges or squares. Serve warm, topped with salsa, sour cream, and/or guacamole.

A spiritual director in the seminary taught us the simple acronym ACTS: daily prayer should include Adoration, Contrition, Thanksgiving, and Supplication. We express our love for God, our sorrow for sins, and our thanks for God's many graces, and finally, ask for God's help for ourselves and others. Praying for others is also known as intercessory prayer. In the next chapter we'll look at grinding grain for flour as an analogy for our prayers on behalf of those who need it most.

Chapter Three
Grinding Grain

Some years ago I gave a lecture on the history of monastic herb gardens at a garden show sponsored by a nursery in Dunlap, Illinois. After my presentation, I met with attendees and signed cookbooks, and a woman came up and said that she had brought me a present. It turned out to be a tabletop flourmill! It was an electric model, using a motorized drive shaft with a moving grindstone pressed up against a stationary one. The wheat goes into a hopper on the top and the freshly ground flour falls into a drawer at the bottom. She said that she had used it a few times but then lost interest, and she thought I would make more use of it. I accepted the gift both sincerely and enthusiastically, although wasn't quite sure how soon I might use it. Little did I know...

Two days later, I found a note from the Academy business manager in my mailbox, telling me that there were five 5-gallon buckets that had just arrived via UPS, with my name on the mailing label. They turned out to be filled with (did you guess it?) whole grain wheat, oats, and soybeans! They were sent from a viewer in Virginia who had bought them from an organic grower and not made use of them as she had expected, so she shipped them to me.

Now I hasten to emphasize that monks are supposed to live simple lives and to avoid acquiring a lot of "things" (I fight a constant battle with clutter in my room!), and we have to ask permission from the abbot or the prior in order to accept gifts. I only mention in this in order to prevent the possibility of a sudden influx of presents from readers. It's not that I don't appreciate the things I have received, but I don't want the abbey to become a clearinghouse for unused kitchen equipment or bumper crops. In this case, however, the arrival of a couple of bushels of whole grain wheat so soon after receiving a flour mill seemed to pass beyond mere coincidence into the realm of Divine Providence.

My flour mill often inspires me to do some intercessory prayer while I'm working. Whenever I use it, I try to remember to pray for the kind woman who gave it to me, which of course made me think of other people in need of prayer. St. Ignatius of Antioch, while on his way to martyrdom in the Coliseum compared himself to Christ's wheat, ground by the teeth of the wild beasts. As I prepared my flour, I think of the people I know ground between the stones of suffering: cracked, crushed, worn down by circumstance. It's hard to judge how much of each grain goes into this batch. I'm baking more by instinct than by measurement, a good thing when you're mixing intercessory prayer in with the dough. It wouldn't do mete out prayer—so much for you, a bit more for her, a little less for them—but rather one ought to be generous, the measuring cup overflowing, the flour of compassion pressed down and shaken together.

I pull the knob on the table top mill and it starts with a grunt, followed by a soft hum as stone spins near stone, the two not quite touching, so the air whispers as it passes between them. I open the hinged lid to reveal the tan plastic hopper, rectangular and slightly sloped towards the hole that feeds the grain between the two stones. When I first received the mill, the hopper was missing, and I had to use a large funnel and a piece of cardboard cut to fit. But about a year later the donor found the hopper while cleaning the garage for a rummage sale, and mailed it to me.

Millet goes in first, the oldest of the cultivated cereals: small, round, straw yellow grains, smaller than rice, smaller than BB's—they fall from the scoop like tow-colored buckshot. Most people today consider millet, literally, for the birds; it's a primary ingredient in bird feed, especially for finches. But H.E. Jacob says that this grain was held in such high esteem in ancient times that it was called "Father Millet." It makes me think of my confreres in the abbey infirmary, priests and brothers who are held in high esteem but who now face the indignities of old age, the gradual dissolution of energy and intellect. Jesus warned Peter, "Amen, amen, I say to you, when you were younger, you used to dress yourself and go where you wanted; but when you grow old, you will stretch out your hands, and someone else will dress you and lead you where you do not want to go." (John 21:18). John comments that this prediction was an indication of Peter's martyrdom, but it always seemed to me as an apt description of anyone weakened by old age. As I pray for my elder confreres, I use a generous scoop, and save some millet to put in whole, for greater texture in the dough.

I twist the dial to move the millstones slightly farther apart—flaxseed next. Flaxseed is full of omega-3 fatty acids (good for your heart, like cold water fish), which are inaccessible unless you grind the seed. Otherwise, the seeds pass right through the digestive system. Slim, chocolate brown seeds with a slippery surface, flaxseeds are so small and hard and slick that one can hardly chop them by hand, although an old-fashioned mortar and pestle does a decent job. A few of my students come to mind, kids with hard shells and slippery psyches, the ones who feign indifference in order to mask their terror, the ones who might pass through a school system if someone didn't take them in hand. They have a father who is alcoholic or a mother who left them or a life that is so normal they know that something must be wrong. They act tough, they act up, they act out—but they can't fool me because I'm the drama director and I teach acting. Sometimes they let me help them, but if not I can always pray. A handful of seeds, another, a tablespoon more, just a few more, round up the strays in the tray: prayer after prayer for these teens, my students, my message in a bottle to a future we cannot see.

Oatmeal next, another twist of the dial. It's my favorite grain in the mix, the one that imparts the best flavor, in addition to having any number of digestive and cardio-vascular benefits. It even feels healthy between my fingers. So prayers for health go into the hopper: for a young man with spina bifida and his courageous mother, for a friend's father who has a cracked vertebra and is in terrible pain, for the newly diagnosed and for those in chemo and for those in remission, for all the sick babies whose parents and grandparents write and e-mail and call the abbey asking for prayer. I pray for those whose illnesses are unknown, evading the doctors' eyes and instruments, and for those who can't afford the health care they need. The mill whirrs and clears its throat with a slight shudder as the last grain goes through.

A few more twists of the dial and I'm ready for the whole wheat grains. I have a supply of wheat flour already ground, but I'd like to add some cracked grains. I adjust the distance between the stones until they are just under the width of a single grain of wheat. Commercial steel rollers can be tuned with such precision that only the shell of the grain (called the bran) is removed, which is what makes my store-bought pure white flour possible. My purpose here is to break the grain into small pieces, to add some crunch to the loaf. But to do that, the wheat is subjected to a jagged violence. The prayers which accompany the wheat are for people who are suffering the most painful breakups, setbacks and betrayals, those who feel their lives are in pieces: a mother of three laid off from work, a classmate who feels his life is without meaning, a college student coping with shame and anger after being raped—those men and women most in need of healing and comfort, for whom the shell of the soul has been rasped raw upon the stone of pain.

As I mentioned near the end of the first, bread baking is a spiritual exercise for Christians in large part because of its association with the Lord's Supper, or "the breaking of the bread" as the Eucharist was called in the early church. One of the earliest extant Christian documents, a first century exhortation known as The Didache, includes a prayer in which the grains gathered from different hillsides is a symbol of both the unity and the diversity of the church:

> As this broken bread was once scattered on the mountains, and after it had been brought together became one, so may thy Church be gathered together from the ends of the earth unto thy kingdom; for thine is the glory, and the power, through Jesus Christ, for ever. (Didache 9:4)[1]

I think of this prayer as I turn off the mill, listening as its humming winds down to a gentle "Amen." I think of gathering all of my prayer intentions into a bowl like grain, ready to mix them into the dough with the less visible but no less real ingredients of love and compassion.

1 The document may be found online at www.carm.org/misc/didache.htm, translation by Charles H. Hoole. The Didache is in the public domain.

You can create your own whole grain blend without having to grind the flours yourself. This recipe features ingredients that are available in most supermarkets.

Father Dom's Whole Grain Mix

Use this blend to replace up to 3 cups of white flour in any two-loaf bread recipe. The bread will have more nutritional value and more fiber as well. Choose a recipe that uses at least some milk as a liquid.

Yield: 3 cups.

1 cup stone-ground whole grain wheat flour
¾ cup stone-ground rye flour
½ cup yellow cornmeal
½ cup quick cooking oats
1 tablespoon of soy flour
1 tablespoon wheat germ
1 tablespoon flaxseed meal
1 tablespoon vital wheat gluten

Whole grain flours absorb more liquid than all-purpose white flour, so you may need less flour overall than what the recipe calls for. Also, whole grain breads require more kneading time (about 25% longer) than white bread recipes. So a recipe that says "knead 6 to 8 minutes" should be kneaded 8 to 10 minutes.

No matter what kind of flour goes into the mixing bowl, our spiritual "loaf" will remain lifeless if we don't have the right kind of yeast. In the next chapter we'll see how the gospel can be the enlivening principle of our lives.

Chapter Four
Yeast: An Enlivening Principle

Ask people with even the slightest experience in the kitchen and they will agree that the number one problem in bread baking is dealing with the yeast. All other mysteries of the kitchen—the perils of pie crust, the risks of boiled rice, the pitfalls of pasta, the riddle of beef roast, the gravy gambit—all pale in comparison to the struggles people have had with 2 1/3 teaspoons (the amount in a single package) of active dry yeast. Evelyn Rabb in her delightful cookbook *The Clueless Baker* puts it this way:

> Yeast is no mere ingredient. It is a living organism. Like a hamster, it requires care and feeding or else it will die. Creepy? Sure, a little. But that's what makes it interesting.[1]

The mystery and magic surrounding yeast is not something new. Yeast has been a mystery to humankind for over 5000 years, starting with the Egyptians who discovered it. An unknown slave in ancient Egypt made a simple batter of Nile water and barley meal, intending to make the same kind of flatbreads that are still made today.[2] But something

---

1 Evelyn Raab, *The Clueless Baker* (Firefly Books, 2001) p. 43.
2 For a complete survey of these breads around the world, see *Flatbreads and Flavors: A Baker's Atlas,* by Jeffrey Alford and

called him away, and he left the batter uncovered. The wild yeast spores in the air fell upon the batter and began to feed, then to multiply. These invisible bacteria broke up the sugars into alcohol and carbolic acid in the process we know as fermentation. The batter became light and fluffy, and doubled in volume.

When the slave returned, he saw the fearful magic that had been visited upon his barley batter, but he feared his master more. So he stirred in some salt, poured the batter onto the flat stone laid over the coals of his kitchen fire and made cakes as he always had. But the resulting flatbreads were lighter and more flavorful than what his master was accustomed to. He was praised for his innovation and urged to repeat it.

Eventually the Egyptians learned to make kneaded breads from a variety of grains and to flavor them with poppy seed, sesame oil, honey, dates and other ingredients. They invented a cone-shaped oven and learned to save a piece of sourdough from the original batch to keep the magic of leavening alive. Baking became an important part of everyday life in Egypt, and bread served as both principal food and customary wages (three loaves of bread and two jugs of beer was the daily dole). The tomb of Rameses is adorned with paintings of the royal bakery, depicting servants kneading a huge trough of dough with their feet, and the dough being shaped into spirals, cones and other more fanciful shapes.

It was not until Van Leeuwenhoek saw yeast cells under his microscope that we began to understand the nature of yeast and the process of fermentation.[3] The yeast that we use for baking today is *Saccharomyces cerevisiae*, which is Latin for "sugar-eating-fungus-for-making-beer." Yeast is a single-cell organism that feeds on sugars (sucrose, fructose, dextrose, etc.) as well as on the starches in flour, and in the process produces carbon dioxide and alcohol. Yeast reproduces by division, so

Naomi Duguid (William Morrow & Co, February 1995).
3 For a more complete description of how active dry yeast is produced, visit *www.breadworld.com,* the Web site of Fleischmann's Yeast.

that a single yeast cell in the presence of a growth medium eventually multiplies into a mighty mass of yeast cells (pay attention; this will be important in a later chapter).

The other word for yeast is leaven, which comes from the same root as "enliven": Yeast gives life to the dough. What was an inert mixture of grain and liquid becomes a living loaf. The yeast then surrenders its life in the process of baking: "In the heat of the oven, the yeasted, living dough dies and gives off a beautiful fragrance to announce its death."[4]

Yeast symbolizes the enlivening principle in our lives, the core values and passions that make our lives worth living. For some people, work is at the center of their identity, so much so that when they retire or are no longer able to work, they lose their sense of self-worth. For others, life is centered on sports or entertainment, or on the acquisition of wealth. Other more positive values like family, creativity and service can be the passions that give our lives meaning. For Christians, however, the yeast in our lives should be the good news of the kingdom.

But just what is this good news? When Jesus began his ministry of preaching, his message was simple: "This is the time of fulfillment. The kingdom of God is at hand. Repent, and believe in the gospel." (Mark 1:15) What is remarkable about this proclamation is its urgency. The Greek word translated as "is at hand" is ηγγικεν, and my college Greek teacher told us it could be translated "has come and is coming and is in your face right now." So one way in which the good news enlivens us is that the kingdom is a *present* reality and not merely the promise of a future reward. Jesus means for us to live lives of fulfillment *now*.

Jesus then invites us to repent, that is, to change our outlook about what fulfillment really is. The Beatitudes found at the beginning of the Sermon on the Mount (Matthew 5:3-11) describe what this new perspective is like. The values of the world are turned upside down. The poor in spirit are blessed, so that we value dependence on God rather than power. In the

4 Robert Pickett, "The Bread of Life" in *Spirit and Life* Vol 97:1 May-June 2001.

kingdom those who mourn are blessed, so we don't avoid all suffering but recognize it as a condition of authentic Christian living. We begin to hunger and thirst for righteousness rather than for wealth or fame. The kingdom values meekness, so we learn that getting our own way all the time doesn't automatically lead to happiness. Jesus' way leads to genuine fulfillment rather than to greater and greater emptiness.

The really good news of the kingdom is that God's love for us is both infinite unconditional. No matter how often we fail to live according to the gospel, our sin cannot make God love us less. Our repentance, our turning back towards God, is a grateful response to a love we can't earn. As one of the prayers of the mass says, "You have no need of our praise, yet our desire to thank you is itself your gift."[5]

When you dissolve dry yeast in warm water with a little sugar, you are "proofing" the yeast; seeing the yeast bubble and foam is proof that it is active. The proof of God's unconditional love is Jesus' self-offering on the cross: "God proves his love for us in that while we were still sinners Christ died for us." (Romans 5:8) Ultimately, the yeast of our lives is the Paschal Mystery. It is the power of the suffering, death and resurrection of Christ at work within us that gives us life, just as yeast gives life to the dough.

Surprisingly, the image of yeast in the Christian Scriptures is primarily a negative one. Early Christianity inherited the Jewish view of leavened breads as a symbol of corruption and decay, since sourdough left too long becomes rotten. Making leavened dough, like wine making, is an exercise in controlled spoilage. Therefore, leavened breads contain an element of decay within them which, to the Hebrew mind, meant that such loaves were unfit to present to God in the daily temple offering known as the "showbread." Although Jewish people ate leavened bread throughout most of the year, yeast breads were also forbidden during the holiest of feasts, the Passover.

This prejudice against leavened bread is evident in several New Testament passages. In Matthew 16:6, Jesus warns the

5 Weekday IV Preface from the Sacramentary.

crowds to "Beware the leaven of the Pharisees," while in Luke 12:1, he specifies that this "leaven" is their hypocrisy, their corrupting influence. Paul's use of the symbolism of yeast in his first letter to the Corinthians is just as negative:

> Your boasting is not appropriate. Do you not know that a little yeast leavens all the dough? Clear out the old yeast, so that you may become a fresh batch of dough, inasmuch as you are unleavened. For our paschal lamb, Christ, has been sacrificed. Therefore let us celebrate the feast, not with the old yeast, the yeast of malice and wickedness, but with the unleavened bread of sincerity and truth. (1Corinthians 5:6-8)

The single instance of a positive view of leavened bread in the Scriptures is the parable of the yeast:

> He spoke to them another parable. "The kingdom of heaven is like yeast that a woman took and mixed with three measures of wheat flour until the whole batch was leavened." (Matthew 13:33)

The usual interpretation of the parable is similar to that given for the parable of the mustard seed: that the kingdom of God starts out small and seemingly insignificant, but eventually grows in importance. However, some commentators have suggested that the parables are much more radical, even subversive.[6] In this view, a parable's purpose is to challenge the religious status quo, such that the core meaning of most of the parables is: "God is not like you thought." The parable of the yeast would have been especially disturbing to his first century audience. All three of the elements of the analogy—the

---

6 For a more complete analysis of the parables as radical stories, see *Parables as Subversive Speech: Jesus as Pedagogue of the Oppressed*, William R. Herzog II (Westminster/John Knox Press, Louisville, Kentucky, 1994).

yeast, the woman, and the amount of flour—would have challenged the theological common sense of the day.[7]

We have already seen how yeast was often considered a symbol of corruption and decay in Jewish tradition, so it would have been shocking for Jesus' audience to hear the kingdom of God to be compared to yeast. His implication seems to be that the new principles of the kingdom of God will challenge traditional views about what is pleasing to God. As we have seen, the Beatitudes and the rest of the Sermon on the Mount seem to bear this out. Jesus calls the poor, the sorrowful, and the persecuted "blessed," a designation that would have been counter-intuitive for people who were taught that God rewarded the virtuous with material prosperity. Jesus also establishes new principles for discipleship and holiness that go beyond the previous standards of the Mosaic Law. He often prefixed his discussion of a traditional teaching with "You have heard it said . . ." followed by a more demanding precept of right living. Jesus' association with sinners and fishermen instead of scribes and Pharisees was a clear sign that the kingdom of God that he announced was going to shake things up.

The second surprise of the parable was the analogy of the activity of God being compared with the homely tasks of a woman. Women in first century Jewish society may have been better off than in some other cultures of the ancient world, but they were still second-rate citizens, considered weak, prone to sin, and in need of the guidance and protection of a father or husband. Throughout the gospels, Jesus is portrayed as treating women with extraordinary respect and compassion. But the parable goes further in depicting the woman as an agent of the kingdom, in her own sphere of influence. This more positive view of women is expressed most fully in Galatians 3:28:

---

7 Although other commentators have written similar analyses, my first encounter with such an interpretation of the parable of the yeast was in "Preaching the Parables of Jesus" (*Church*, Winter 1992; pp. 19-24) by Dr. Richard Stern.

"There is neither Jew nor Greek, there is neither slave nor free person, there is not male or female, for you are all one in Christ Jesus."

The amount of flour is the most surprising element of the parable, which is not entirely evident in most English translations. "Three measures" is the usual translation for the original Greek τρια σατα, which is a little over a *bushel* of flour (1.125 bushels, to be precise). That's a ridiculously large amount of flour—you'd need a 100-quart Hobart mixer with a dough hook as big as your leg to knead it! Translating into kitchen measures, 1.125 bushels is 144 cups of flour. Presuming we used a common recipe for basic white bread that uses 5 ½ cups of flour, 144 cups is enough to make 26 batches of bread of two loaves each, giving us a total of 52 loaves, each weighing about a pound and a half. If we're frugal but not stingy, we can get 16 slices out of a loaf, yielding 832 slices, enough for 416 peanut butter and jelly sandwiches (we'd need 33 jars of jelly, and 64 of peanut butter).

What's the message of the story? It's simple: The kingdom of heaven is like a woman who wants to do more than feed her family. The kingdom announced by Jesus is like a woman who wants to feed the village. The kingdom of God is like a woman who wants to feed the world. The kingdom is for *everybody*.

The kingdom of God is like the seventy-five-year-old woman who made a small loaf of bread (nearly 100 of them) for every person who attended a talk I gave to her parish Altar and Rosary Society. The kingdom of God is like the monks at Saint Joseph's Abbey in Louisiana, whose "Pennies for Bread" program provides about 1,750 loaves of fresh homemade bread every week to food programs in their area.[8] The kingdom of God is like Bread for the World, an organization

---

8 For information on supporting the monks of Saint Joseph Abbey in their ministry, call the abbey at (985) 892-1800, or write to: P.B.A. Manager, Pennies for Bread and the Abbey, Saint Joseph Abbey, Saint Benedict, Louisiana 70457. Their Web site is www.stjosephabbey.org.

that successfully lobbies for changes in legislation and public policy to support food programs in the U.S. and abroad.[9]

The parable of the yeast is not only a story that shocked people 2,000 years ago—it continues to challenge us today. As I dissolve yeast into warm water and stir in sugar and flour, questions rise from the bowl like the earthy scent of the leavened dough:

- Am I consciously mixing in the yeast of the kingdom into my life, or do I wait for wild yeast to "drop out of the sky" before I let the Good News change my life?

- Am I mixing in the right leaven, or is it corrupt, hypocritical, even dead? Do my actions match my words, am I the same on the inside as I am on the outside?

- Am I allowing God to work through others, especially those who are different from me? Do I refuse to be influenced by people of a different gender or race or economic status?

- Is my spirituality life-giving for others, or am I only concerned with nourishing myself? What level of commitment do I have for those who are hungry for food, and those who are hungry for love?

Yeast's amazing powers of expansion don't work only on kneaded dough, but also for batter breads, many of which require less time to prepare. Better still, you can make the stand mixer do most of the work for you! My mother made this Streamlined White Bread recipe often when we were growing up, and since the publication of the first edition of this

---

9 For information on how to join Bread for the World, write to Bread for the World, 50 F Street, NW, Suite 500, Washington, DC 20001 or call 800-82-BREAD. Their Web address is www. bread.org.

book, many mothers have told me that it has become a family favorite. I hope it will become one of your favorites too.

Streamlined White Bread

Yield: 1 loaf

1 package active dry yeast
1 ¼ cups warm water
2 tablespoons vegetable oil
1 teaspoon salt
2 tablespoons granulated sugar
3 cups all-purpose flour, divided

Sprinkle yeast over warm water in medium bowl; stir to dissolve. Let stand until foamy. Add oil, salt, sugar and half of the flour. Using a heavy wooden spoon, beat 300 strokes (or beat on medium speed of electric mixer about 2 minutes). Add remaining flour and stir until thoroughly incorporated. Cover bowl with a clean cloth and let rise in a warm, draft-free place about 30 minutes, or until doubled.

Beat the batter about 25 strokes, then spread evenly in a lightly greased 9X5X3-inch loaf pan. Let rise, uncovered, 30-40 minutes, or until the batter just reaches the top of the pan. (Do not allow to over-rise or the bread will collapse during cooling.)

Bake in a preheated 375-degree oven 45-50 minutes, or until the loaf is browned and sounds hollow when tapped on the bottom. Let cool on wire rack.

Christmas 1961, at age 14 months, with my brother Marty and sister Angela. My resemblance to the Pillsbury Doughboy is already in evidence, thanks to my mother's baking.

Yeast is only effective when it is mixed into the dough and kneaded thoroughly. In the same way the enlivening principle of the Good News must permeate our lives. But how can we incorporate the values of the gospel into our lives? We begin with the spiritual mixing and kneading of meditation and prayer.

Chapter Five
Mixing And Kneading

When you begin the process of mixing ingredients for bread and kneading the dough, something remarkable is taking place on the molecular level. Two protein molecules (glutenin and gliadin) found in wheat flour combine with water to form a stretchy protein molecule called gluten. In the process of mixing and kneading, this miraculous molecule stretches out and wraps around itself to form a flexible web of protein, acting as a net to capture the carbon dioxide produced by the yeast in the process of consuming sugars. The net is actually visible if you roll the dough out thin and hold it up to the light—in well-kneaded dough, it looks like lace. Without this infrastructure of gluten molecules, the carbon dioxide escapes through the surface of the dough, and the bread will not rise.

What is most remarkable about this whole process is that it is virtually invisible, since it takes place on the molecular level. As you mix and knead, you can't see the glutenin and gliadin bond with water to form the all-important gluten, nor is it possible to watch the individual protein strands wrap around and connect with each other to form the gluten network. But after six or eight or ten minutes of vigorous kneading, there is an obvious difference in the dough. It becomes lively, supple and smooth. The dough has an inner resilience that allows it to hold its shape when it rises and bakes free-form on a baking sheet and that keeps it from spilling over the sides of a loaf pan in the heat of the oven.

In the spiritual life, daily meditation and prayer are the activities that develop a similar interior resilience in the believer. By "mixing and kneading" the gospel of Christ into our lives through the daily discipline of reading and reflection, a spiritual infrastructure is formed, slowly and invisibly, that helps us to "hold our shape," that is, maintain our identity as Christians regardless of exterior conditions.

One of the frustrations expressed by people in the early stages of beginning to pray is that "it seems like nothing is happening." Despite a daily commitment to prayer and regular reading of the Bible and other spiritual texts, they feel as though they have not been significantly changed by the experience. "I don't expect God to speak to me directly," a friend of mine told me, "but I'd like to think that prayer would *change* me somehow."

But the changes that take place in the believer are like the changes in the dough during kneading: they occur inside of us, sometimes at an infinitesimal level of the heart, in some small and secret part of the soul that confounds calibration or measurement. Connections are being made, like that between the molecules of protein and water, that we cannot immediately perceive—but those connection are real, and they have a cumulative effect as long as we are faithful to the daily discipline of prayer.

Dedication to prayer is not easy. Sometimes prayer seems repetitive, boring, even physically exhausting. In addition to daily Mass at Saint Bede Abbey, we pray together at least three times a day using the Book of Psalms as our primary text. We go through the full psalter every two weeks, which means that at the time of this writing, I have prayed each of the psalms 234 times. I'm not bragging—many of my confreres could double or triple that number! Faithfulness to daily prayer requires a certain level of spiritual stamina and perseverance even when it seems "nothing is happening."

One never knows when those tiny connections may coalesce into a genuine insight or personal revelation. Recently I was meditating on the temptation in the desert (Matthew 4:1-

11). Jesus has fasted in the Judean wilderness for forty days, and the devil visits him in his weakness. "If you are the Son of God," Satan urges, "command that these stones become loaves of bread." I had heard, read and prayed about this passage many times with the understanding that the devil is tempting Jesus to use his power for personal comfort. On this particular day, I realized that the temptation lay not only in Jesus' immediate physical hunger, but in the more dangerous belief that *all* hungers should be *immediately* satisfied. The desire for instant gratification is a greater temptation than the desire for bread. Like Esau selling his birthright for a bowl of stew, we risk losing our divine birthright in exchange for the pleasure of the moment. Making that small connection in meditation led to another 30 minutes of reflection and a full page in my journal.

Familiarity with Scripture through daily meditation also makes biblical references arise during other activities. I have already written of how Scripture passages about bread come to mind in the kitchen, but the same thing happens at other times. When I fly kites with a friend and his children, I'm reminded of Psalm 139:8: "If I ascend to the heavens, you are there." When I feel anxious about a friend who is seriously ill, I take comfort from Psalm 41:4: "The LORD sustains them on their sickbed, allays the malady when they are ill." I've even heard this sort of biblical sub-referencing during a monastic game of volleyball. One monk cheerfully threatened his confrere on the other side of the net, and his opponent replied with a promise to spike the ball, accompanied by a quote from Psalm 81:11: "Open wide your mouth that I may fill it!"

Several years ago, one of our Academy students was dying of a rare form of bone cancer. Jenny had been receiving various treatments, standard and experimental, for the past four years, but with little success. In freshman religion, we decided to make cards with Scripture verses on them, and one young man chose 2 Corinthians 4:16: "Therefore we are not discouraged. Rather, though our outer self is wasting away, our inner self is being renewed day by day." One can hardly imagine a better passage to share with a classmate afflicted with terminal cancer. The week before my student died, she made her good-byes to her friends, calling them in one by one to speak with each girl alone, and many students visited her all week. Two of our faculty members were present when she died. The nurse said that at the end, Jenny opened her eyes, smiled and whispered, "Wonderful!" just before her heart stopped. Her outer, physical nature had wasted away completely, but I have faith that her soul had been completely renewed by the power of Jesus' resurrection.

How can we ensure that such powerful texts will be available to our memories when we need them? What most people need is a simple technique for reading the Bible in a prayerful way, one which promotes both familiarity with the text and understanding its significance in one's life. One method that has long been a part of monastic tradition is *lectio divina* (LEX-ee-oh duh-VEE-nah, or *lectio* for short). This four-part process has been gaining in popularity in recent years, and several excellent books have been written on the subject.[1] Lectio divina has four simple steps: *lectio* (reading), *meditatio* (reflection), *oratio* (prayer) and *contemplatio* (listening in silence). Here are some general guidelines for each step:

- **Lectio** For this first stage, find a comfortable place to sit where you can be undisturbed. Choose a passage from the Bible. It can be short or long, but I recommend that it be no more than a chapter. In the Gospels, a single story or parable is sufficient. Read the passage slowly, with reverence—you might read out loud once, and then silently several times. Give the words a chance to sink in, that is, make sure you *listen* as you read. The point is not to gain information through study, but to make contact with the Living Word.

1 *Sacred Reading: The Ancient Art of Lectio Divina* by Michael Casey (Triumph Books; April 1996) is especially recommended by a number of my fellow monks at Saint Bede Abbey.

- **Meditatio** The word "meditation" can be daunting, but in fact it's nothing more than finding a word, phrase or verse that speaks to you in a special way, and then repeating it mentally or aloud. This is the step that is most like kneading bread—we repeat the passage in order to make connections. It may be that the reading evokes happy or painful memories, or addresses an area of your life in need of healing or growth. The goal of meditation is to discover how the passage is speaking to you today. If you find yourself being distracted by other thoughts or anxieties, bring them into your meditation: Does the passage illuminate your worries? I never feel guilty about distractions at prayer anymore; I deliberately incorporate them into my reflection. I figure if it's important to me, it's important to God. Some people, myself included, use a prayer journal to reflect on the passage through writing, which helps keep one focused.
- **Oratio** Your meditation will lead you naturally to prayer: prayers of praise, thanksgiving, petition. It may be that your meditation has suggested a person in particular need of intercessory prayer, or you may be challenged by the reading to ask forgiveness for past sins and for help in the future. No matter what the topic is, try to avoid memorized prayers; instead, speak from your own heart. You don't have to be clever or profound, just honest.
- **Contemplatio** In this final step of lectio divina, we rest in silence, open to the presence of God. If distractions occur during this step, we should gently dismiss them and try to calm our thoughts. Contemplation is the most difficult step for many people, because it requires one to wait in patience. However, without this step, we run the risk of making our prayer something we do solely by our own power, without acknowledging God's sovereignty.

This description does not begin to express how meaningful the practice of lectio can be. In fact, as I composed the previous sentence, I had considered a wide variety of adjectives to describe it: beautiful, profound, life-giving, transforming, awesome, unbearably cool, etc. Once I introduced lectio divina to a class of juniors, expecting them to resist any activity that required so much silence. We took nearly the entire period to get through the exercise, using Ephesians 4:1-6 as our text. Much to my surprise, at the end of the period they all said it was one of the best experiences of prayer they had ever had. One young man enthused, "I came in all stressed out about tests and homework, and I felt like God was sitting right next to me, telling me that I'd do OK."

My young student later explained that he didn't experience God's comfort in words but in feelings. You might wonder if you will hear the voice of God speaking to you in the silence of contemplation. I confess I have only had that experience once, briefly, when I prayed in the Blessed Sacrament Chapel before I took my first vows as a monk. When I shared my story with a religious sister who had been in vows for over 50 years she said, "Well, you're one up on me, Father!" I have no doubt that her spiritual life was far advanced compared to mine, but her prayer had been undramatic, as it is for most of us, most of the time. We reflect and pray and listen, and the insights we receive are gifts of the Holy Spirit, sometimes as wordless certainties that only the heart can interpret. It is generally agreed that "hearing voices" is not a good goal for prayer.

When I teach lectio divina at a workshop or retreat, I'm often asked how long the process should take. The time spent on any one step will vary from day to day. Sometimes a single reading of the text will grab hold of us, and we might linger over a single word or phrase for half an hour before moving on to reflection and prayer. Some days we are inspired to pray for a long period, while on other days resting in silent contemplation will take the bulk of our prayer time. As a general rule, I think one should dedicate at least 20 minutes a day to lectio.

As with any new spiritual exercise, it may take a while to get comfortable with this method of prayer and meditation, but be patient with yourself. You may be surprised at the insights you discover within your own heart and how clearly Sacred Scripture can speak to your everyday life. One advantage to lectio is that it is easily adaptable to each person, regardless of one's experience—you 'knead" at your own pace. In *Prayer and Temperament*,[2] a book about finding prayer forms suited to different personalities, the authors recommend lectio divina as an appropriate prayer form for all Christians, regardless of their background and disposition.

The biggest obstacle for many people is choosing what passages of the Bible to read. "All scripture is inspired by God and profitable for teaching, for reproof, for correction, and for training in righteousness" (2 Timothy 3:16), but not every chapter of the Bible is equally accessible for those who are just beginning to practice lectio divina. Here are some suggested passages to get you started:

Genesis 50:15-21 Joseph's brothers plead for forgiveness
Joshua 24:14-18 The renewal of the covenant
Psalm 1 A description of the just person
Psalm 150 A hymn of praise to God
Isaiah 6:1-8 The call of Isaiah
Jeremiah 18:1-10 The lesson of the potter

Matthew 25:31-46 The final judgment
Mark 7:24-30 A woman's faith
Luke 12:16-21 The parable of the rich fool
John 13:31-35 The New Commandment
Colossians 3:12-17 The virtues of a believer

---

2 Chester P. Michael and Mary C. Norrisy, *Prayer and Temperament: Different Prayer Forms for Different Personality Types* (Open Door; revised edition, December 1991). The book is based on the psychology of the Meyers-Briggs Type Indicator and offers sample lectio exercises for the four basic personality types of the MBTI.

Like the woman in the parable of the yeast, my Grandma Tootsie was someone who wanted to feed everybody. As a result, there was a constant stream of visitors at her home. To keep family, friends, weekend guests supplied with fresh baked goods, Grandma would mix up the following refrigerator roll dough. It makes a lot of dough, and she'd take out just enough for a small batch of cinnamon rolls or buns for dinner, saving the rest for the next meal. The dough will keep for two or three days in the fridge. The original recipe, which I have adapted somewhat, came from her sister Jo Rita. The long rising period in the "icebox" gives the rolls exquisite flavor, which proves that sometimes a longer period of rest can make us better hosts as well!

Grandma Tootsie   **...and the rolls she inspired.**

Grandma Tootsie's Refrigerator Rolls

Yield: About 2 ½ dozen dinner rolls.

1 ¼ cups hot water
1 cup milk
½ cup granulated sugar
2 packages active dry yeast
2 teaspoons salt
2 tablespoons vegetable oil
2 eggs, well beaten
7 to 8 cups all-purpose flour, divided

Combine hot water, milk and sugar in large bowl; stir until sugar is dissolved. Let cool to lukewarm. Sprinkle yeast over milk mixture; stir to dissolve. Let stand 10 minutes. Add salt, oil and eggs; stir thoroughly. Add 6 cups of the flour, 2 cups at a time, mixing after each addition until flour is thoroughly incorporated. Add enough of the remaining flour, about ½ cup at a time, to make a soft dough that is slightly sticky.

Turn out dough onto lightly floured surface. Knead 3 or 4 minutes, lightly sprinkling the dough with flour to keep the dough manageable. Do not over-knead; the dough should remain soft and will not spring back quite as much as for bread dough.

Place dough in a clean bowl, lightly brush top of dough with vegetable oil, and cover with plastic wrap. Let rise for 1 hour before using, or store in refrigerator for up to three days.

For dinner rolls, form balls of dough about the size of a golf ball and place balls in lightly greased muffin tins. Cover with a clean, dry cloth and let rise in a warm draft-free place 60 to 90 minutes, or until doubled.

Bake rolls in a preheated 425-degree oven 12 to 15 minutes, or until browned. Serve warm.

To read. To reflect. To pray. To listen in silence. These spiritual "mixing and kneading" activities require sustained concentration and effort if we are to make connections between Scripture and our lives. But the next step in bread making offers us an even greater challenge: to do nothing.

Chapter Six
Letting It Rest

Most yeast bread recipes include a period of "proofing" the dough, that is, letting it rest in a warm place, free of drafts, usually covered with a clean dish towel. The purpose of the resting period is to allow the process of fermentation to take place. In a warm environment, with plenty of sugars and starches to consume, the yeast cells multiply as they release the carbon dioxide that makes the dough rise.

Let the dough rise long enough, and the gases will begin to escape from the surface of the dough. If the dough was lightly oiled just before the rising period, you can actually see the bubbles form and hear the whisper of the dough as it "exhales." When my brother Vincent was about three, he lifted up the towel covering a bowl of risen dough, and bent his little ear down to listen. "Mom!" he called excitedly with a toddler's pronunciation, "It breathe-ez!"

At the same time the yeast is at work, the grains of flour continue to absorb liquid, thereby making the dough softer and more supple. The gluten network, which can become stiff during the process of kneading, also relaxes. Even recipes using fast-rising yeast require at least ten minutes of rest after kneading to allow the mixture to coalesce into a workable mass of dough.

The principle of the "Sabbath rest" is an important part of biblical spirituality, as essential in Christian living as in baking. Marva J. Dawn in her insightful book *Keeping the*

Sabbath Wholly notes that the Sabbath rest reminds us that we cannot provide for ourselves and that even the prayerful activities we associate with Sunday are a gift from God. "If we are to feast spiritually, God must provide the manna of his Word. Only by his grace has he chosen to reveal himself to us; only by his grace can we understand and believe what his revelation declares."[1]

I won't waste time beating society over the head with the guilt hammer for treating Sunday as the day to get all the chores done you neglected last week. I would offer this prophetic witness: at Saint Bede Abbey, we have a high school, a print shop, 1,000 acres of land, and a huge complex to maintain, but the prior won't give anyone permission to go to town on errands on Sunday, nor will you find monks hoeing in the gardens or repairing plumbing aside from an emergency. In spite of all this Sabbath inactivity, everything seems to get done. For myself, I may prune the herbs in the garden on a Sunday so I can make Italian Onion Herb Bread for supper, but I won't pull weeds.

Sometimes people are surprised to hear that monks play cards or watch sports on TV or engage in any number of recreational activities like "normal" people. But monks need relaxation time as much as anyone. St. Augustine spoke of "holy leisure," and in his rule St. Benedict allows time for rest and relaxation, even naps. One sometimes hears an old joke describing a monk as "someone who gets up at 5 o'clock— twice a day!"

The best illustration of the monastic principle of relaxation is from *The Sayings of the Desert Fathers*,[2] a collection of sayings and stories from the monks who lived in the Egyptian desert in the fourth and fifth century. Once a hunter came upon Abbot Anthony relaxing with the brothers. The hunter

1 Marva J. Dawn, *Keeping the Sabbath Wholly: Ceasing, Resting, Embracing, Feasting* (Eerdman's, Grand Rapids, Michigan, 1989) p. 158.
2 *The Sayings of the Desert Fathers* (Cistercian Publications, revised edition, 1987).

was shocked to see them just sitting around. The abbot said to him, "Put an arrow in your bow and shoot it." The hunter did so. Then Anthony said, "Shoot another," and again the hunter complied. Then the old man said, "Shoot yet again." The hunter objected, "If I keep bending my bow I will break it." Abbot Anthony replied, "It is the same with God's work. If we stretch the brothers continually, without measure, they will soon break. So sometimes we must relax to meet their needs."

The wisdom of the ancient monastics is as pertinent today as it was in the fourth century. We all need time for rest and relaxation, time for "holy leisure." Unfortunately, we often fill our free time with more busy-ness—clubs, sports, meetings, hobbies, activities of various sorts—all of them good in themselves, but not if they keep us from ever slowing down. I'm guilty of this tendency as much as anyone, which is why I appreciate baking bread so much. It makes me slow down, stick around in one place longer and spend quality time with my confreres, my family, my friends and my students. Periodically in the course of making bread, one has to let the dough rest. The same is true for the baker.

I like to write in my bread journal during the time that the dough is rising. I also keep another journal for relating the events of the day and reflecting on their meaning, but my bread journal only comes out at the kitchen table. It holds ideas for new recipes, notes about possible topics for future lectures and demonstrations, and accounts of successes and failures in the kitchen. I also use it to explore the spiritual significance of bread—in my life and in the life of the monastic community, in Scripture and in history. Many of the reflections in my bread journal have evolved into homilies, retreat conferences and even some of the chapters in this book. Noah ben Shea has written a charming book about a baker named Jacob who writes inspirational verses to tuck into his loaves:

He turned on the mixer and began to work the
first dough. His eyes followed the spiral metal arm on
its endless roll. Its pattern confirmed a truth he saw

everywhere.

Gradually, he added the warm water, careful not to make the dough too stiff or too wet. Moderation. Balance. Taking measure of what he was doing.

Jacob the baker understood this.

Now there was time. His time. A little time. The dough needed to rise. The oven's heat curled through the bakery.

Jacob took a thick flat pencil from his back pocket and began to write...[3]

Granted, writing is not the same thing as resting, but I do find it relaxing. Writing often helps me to feel the presence of God in the midst of my activity. But I have to be careful not to turn journaling into just another job on my list of "things to achieve today," or it may prove to be an obstacle to intimacy with God. The gospel story of Mary and Martha (Luke 10:38-42) illustrates how even a Christian virtue like hospitality can be a barrier to recognizing the presence of the Lord.

As they continued their journey he [Jesus] entered a village where a woman whose name was Martha welcomed him. She had a sister named Mary [who] sat beside the Lord at his feet listening to him speak. Martha, burdened with much serving, came to him and said, "Lord, do you not care that my sister has left me by myself to do the serving? Tell her to help me." The Lord said to her in reply, "Martha, Martha, you are anxious and worried about many things. There is need of only one thing. Mary has chosen the better part and it will not be taken from her."

Martha's complaint may be nothing more than sibling rivalry, or a genuine desire to be with Jesus. But I think it more likely that the real root of her problem is the fear that her

---

3 Noah benShea, *Jacob the Baker* (Ballantine Books, 1989) pp. 6-7.

serving will seem inadequate. But her passion for hospitality is misplaced; she's so busy in the kitchen that she has forgotten her guest. Jesus confirms that the details of service are sometimes to be laid aside for sake of sitting at the feet of the Lord and listening to his gentle instruction.

Martha had the opportunity to spend time with Jesus in an intimate setting—how many in the crowds of Galilee or Jerusalem would have begged for such an opportunity! We are far more fortunate: The Spirit of Jesus, the Holy Spirit which came to dwell with us at baptism, ensures the Lord's permanent availability to us. The bread of hospitality and fellowship is rising quietly, the one thing that is necessary. Jesus is near, he has emptied his schedule. Alone in the room, he beckons us: "Come away by yourselves to a deserted place and rest awhile" (Mark 6:31).

If you decide to nap while your dough does the same, be sure to set your alarm just in case. But if you absolutely can't nap or "do nothing," here is a modest list of acceptable substitutes.

THINGS TO DO WHILE WAITING
FOR THE BREAD TO RISE

- Call your best friend and invite her to come over for fresh bread. Ask her to bring her favorite flavor of jam.

- Write to the person who taught you to bake or gave you the recipe you're using: "Thanks for giving me the gift of an hour of rest."

- Go to the backyard and pick a small vase of flowers— resist the temptation to pull weeds. Look at each flower carefully; appreciate the variation of colors in each petal, the texture of its leaves, and the scent of both the bloom and the cut stem. As you arrange the flowers, pray in thanksgiving to the Creator for the wonderful variety of living beings on the earth.

- Have a cup of herb tea and listen to folk music, especially harp, hammered dulcimer, fiddle and bass. If you get really inspired, put a dish towel on your head and dance in the living room.

- Since most bread recipes make two loaves, decide which of your neighbors will get the second loaf. Find a nice basket to put it in when you deliver it.

- If you start to feel guilty for not working, lie down until the feeling goes away. Remind yourself that you are not doing nothing, you are making bread. After all, one does not stop being a parent just because the baby is taking a nap.

- Page through a cookbook and decide what kind of bread you will make next and when. Perhaps you might choose a religious festival or personal holiday to celebrate. Mark the day you have chosen on the calendar in red, so you have something to look forward to.

- Get out an old photo album and look at pictures of your family. Ask God to give each one whatever grace he or she lacks the most right now, without being specific—God knows better than you do what they need! Just lift them up to the Lord in gratitude and love.

- Do one of the lectio divina exercises from the previous chapter. Be sure to leave plenty of time for the last step, *contemplatio*: listening in silence for God's reply.

- Toward the end of the rising period, raise up the towel covering the bowl and listen to the dough breathe.

On a recent Sunday I did indeed go out and prune in my garden, and came back with several Mason jars filled with fragrant herbs. I knew that we were getting a pasta dish for supper the next night, so I created this recipe on the spot.

Italian Herbal Swirl

Dough
2 cups warm water
2 packages dry yeast
1 tsp. salt
¼ cup olive oil
½ cup stone ground cornmeal
5 to 5 ½ cups bread flour

Filling
1 cup ricotta cheese
¼ cup fresh oregano leaves
½ cup fresh parsley leaves
½ cup fresh basil leaves
1 cup snipped chives
salt and pepper

NOTE: All herbs should be loosely packed when measured.

Put water into a large bowl. Add yeast, stir to dissolve. Add salt, oil and cornmeal and beat well. Add 4 cups of flour, one cup at a time, mixing thoroughly each time until flour is thoroughly incorporated and beat well. Work in enough of remaining flour to form a soft dough. Knead for 6 to 8 minutes. Place in large bowl and cover with a dish towel. Let rise in a warm place free from drafts for about one hour, or until doubled in volume.

Coarsely chop parsley, oregano and basil leaves and

toss together with the chives until mixed. Punch dough down and knead briefly. Divide in half, and roll each half into a rectangle 12 inches wide and 14 inches high. Spread ½ cup of ricotta evenly over each half of the dough and sprinkle on chopped herbs. Sprinkle lightly with salt and pepper. Roll up jelly-roll style and place seam side down on parchment on an 11X15 - inch baking sheet. Cover with a dry towel and let rise until nearly doubled, about 30 minutes. Make 5 diagonal slashes with a sharp knife or razor blade on the top of each loaf. Bake at 400 degrees F. for 15 to 20 minutes. Bread is done when lightly browned and sounds hollow when tapped. Cool on racks.

Once the dough has rested and risen, the baker punches it down and kneads it vigorously. Why this sudden, violent transition from a warm, restful place to the cold, hard countertop? In the next chapter we'll find out why it's necessary for the dough (and for us) to be punched down.

Chapter Seven
Being Punched Down

As I described in previous chapters (hope you were paying attention!), during the dough's period of rest the yeast cells reproduce by dividing again and again, forming masses of cells throughout the dough. But the cells at the center of these clumps of yeast soon stop growing. Surrounded by other cells, they no longer have access to nourishment and go dormant. The clusters of yeast must be broken up and re-distributed throughout the dough in order for the bread to rise evenly during the final proof and while they are in the oven.

The means by which the baker achieves this redistribution of the yeast is to punch the dough down—vigorously—and knead it again. Sometimes I even raise the dough over my head with both hands and slam it down on the counter, which not only makes a satisfactory *whump* but also is a good warm-up for the kneading that follows. Thus the yeast is no longer in isolated pockets, but permeates the dough "like the leaven of divine justice," as the Rule of St. Benedict says.

We saw earlier how yeast is an enlivening principle, a symbol of the gospel values that should permeate every aspect of our lives. Unfortunately, we can become complacent in the spiritual life, spending too much time in a warm, comfortable place that doesn't challenge us to further growth. Our faith can go dormant, like the yeast cells at the center of the clump. As a result, we isolate the gospel into separate pockets in our lives, without allowing it to influence everyday decisions and actions.

There are many examples of separating faith from practice: going to church on Sunday but not acknowledging God's presence the rest of the week; professing to be a Christian while failing to apply gospel values to one's business policies; enjoying the benefits of membership in one's parish or church without volunteering for the congregation's various activities; "saying" prayers rather than truly praying them. We're often Christians with good intentions and weak convictions, wanting to *be* good without wanting to make the effort to *become* good.

This spiritual complacency is dangerous, because in order for the divine leaven to be re-distributed, it may be necessary for us to be punched down. A public humiliation, a financial setback, a failed relationship—all of these experiences can have the effect of forcing us to growing spiritually, to be mindful of our radical need for God every day at every moment, and to take steps to incorporate our Christian faith into everyday life.

I would like to offer some reflections on two personal experiences of being punched down. I confess that neither of these stories can compare with the anguish of being laid off from work or being betrayed by a friend. I've never been denied a job because of my gender nor been oppressed because of my skin color, and the occasional slights I have received because of my Catholicism don't amount to more than a blister long since healed. Nonetheless, I hope my reflections on my own experiences can help to illuminate the times when you have been punched down by life.

My first example is more comic than tragic, but it illustrates what happens when one concentrates so much on personal growth that the obligation to help others is forgotten. When I first joined the monastery, I was assigned to help Br. Francis with his prayer book at Divine Office (the daily round of monastic prayer). Br. Francis had had a stroke that caused both memory loss and a shortened attention span. His failure to care for his diabetes had resulted in poor vision and the amputation of his left foot just below the knee. Our prayer books at that time were somewhat complex, requiring the monks to flip back and forth between various sections, so my novice master suggested that Br. Francis needed "a little help" keeping on track.

"A little help" turned out to mean constant vigilance throughout the entire course of the service. I would push Br. Francis to the chapel in his wheelchair and settle him in the aisle next to my choir stall. Then I would set his book to the correct page and try to concentrate on my own prayer, only to find that Br. Francis had, for no discernible purpose, turned to another section and gotten befuddled. Or he couldn't see well enough to tell what verse of the hymn was being sung, and I'd have to point to the correct line. Or he would drop the book and pages would actually fall out, so I'd have to spend time sorting them before handing the book back. As someone just learning how to pray the Divine Office myself, these constant distractions became increasingly irritating (but from hindsight, so minor that I blush to recall my frustration).

The last straw came one autumn afternoon when I took Br. Francis outside for a tour of the grounds, so he could enjoy the bright colors of the leaves and the sunlight on the huge pumpkins growing in the vegetable garden. Then we went inside for a cup of coffee. As we sat at the coffee corner, I was feeling quite smug for being so nice to my poor, elderly confrere, when Br. Francis turned to me and said, "Say, maybe you can tell me—who is that guy who helps me with my book at Office?"

I was dumbfounded, speechless! Br. Francis evidently mistook my silence for stupidity and elaborated, "You know—that big guy with the moustache. What's his name?" Here I was spending the majority of my prayer time helping him keep the book straight, and he had no idea who I was. My resentment made me try a little test. "I don't know, brother," I said between clenched teeth. "Is that Br. Dominic?" His reply? "Oh no—I know *him*."

I practically flew upstairs to my novice master's office to complain about the injustice of this situation. I didn't shout or pound the desk, but I did wave my arms a lot and point in the general direction of the coffee klatch. My religious superior listened politely until I came to my indignant conclusion: "Father, if I have to help him with his book, I can't pray very well!" He smiled gently and replied, "Yes, brother—but if you don't help him with his book, he can't pray at all."

Whump! The over-risen dough of my self-importance slammed onto the kitchen counter of old age and the realities of monastic life. I think I left the room without another word. Shortly thereafter I was assigned to help Br. Francis take his daily bath and care for his prosthetic foot, a service not without its frustrations, but which I undertook with considerably more humility. I'd been punched down, but the gospel value

of compassion had been redistributed and leavened my labors on his behalf.

It is ironic that Br. Francis suffered much of his disability because of diabetes, since that was the catalyst for my second (more serious) experience of being punched down. For a couple of weeks in early November 1995, I developed the classic diabetic symptoms: constant thirst, frequent urination (about every twenty minutes, and five times a night), and eventually, blurred vision. I recognized the symptoms for what they were, and went to the doctor on November fourteenth. My blood sugar was a staggering 675 (about 120 to 140 is normal—the nurse was astounded that I was both coherent and conscious). So at age 35 I got a glucometer, an 1800-calorie diet, a twice-daily prescription, and a faith crisis.

Health care professionals say that for many people, discovering that you are diabetic is rather like experiencing the stages of grief: denial, anger, bargaining, etc. In my case, I leap-frogged over denial and went directly to anger. I was both surprised and frightened by the strength of my rage, which seems especially silly now after years of living with diabetes. But at the time I was furious at God for giving me this cross, to the point that I refused to sing or respond at mass, or even to receive communion for a whole week. After all, I had given up smoking earlier that year in September and God gave me diabetes just in time for the holidays. Like I didn't have enough rules in monastic life, so now I had to memorize starch exchanges?!

Eventually I realized that I had to resolve my feelings about my condition, because I was scheduled to celebrate the first Sunday of Advent at a nearby parish. I didn't want to stand up in front of the congregation and mouth platitudes about God's love and God's plan when I wasn't too convinced of God's justice. So I turned to the readings for that Sunday, hoping to find a sentence or phrase that would speak to my situation.

The theme running throughout the readings of the day was Christ's coming, both at Christmas and at the end of time. I didn't find anything that moved me until I reached the last line of the gospel: "The Son of Man will come at a time when you least expect it." The words leaped off the page and burned in my mind like the Christmas star. Christ was coming to me at a time and in a way I never expected—in weakness and dependence, as startling and mysterious as his nativity. It was as though I could hear him saying, "Dominic, I would speak now a new language of love, and you will be years in learning it. The helplessness of my infancy I will bring to birth in your own body. I give you weakness so you will have health and strength, a share in my cross so you will have fullness of life."

That Sunday I preached about my experience of anger and reconciliation to the people of the parish and was surprised by the outpouring of support and compassion I received. One of the Sunday school teachers had her students make cards for me. One of them had a doughnut with a circle/slash drawn through it—"Just say no to the BIG O" was the caption. Another little girl wrote: "You Can Do It!!! It will be hard but that's what God wants"—out of the mouths of babes. Others urged me to "Give God another chance" and to "stay in shape and don't get temtachions [sic] and other things." I kept them on the coffee table in my office to keep me inspired throughout the day.

So I spent Advent trying to let the Divine break into my life in new ways and learning how to eat healthy in a season of excess. Two days after I received my diagnosis, a huge platter of doughnuts appeared at the breakfast table, with a glazed cinnamon roll the size of my head at the apex of the mound. I whimpered, bit my knuckle and turned firmly toward the shredded wheat. I thought that perhaps sprinkling Grape Nuts on top would improve the gustatory experience, but the result was like eating a soggy bale of hay with little rocks mixed in. Nevertheless, I have managed to integrate the diabetic diet into my monastic lifestyle, despite occasional "temtachions and other things."

In the intervening years, I have come to realize what my distress was really about: limiting my *consumption*. The purpose of monastic discipline is to teach the monk to control his appetites, to regulate the desire for food, for sex, for personal comfort and material possession, so that none of them can threaten to take the place of God. It took a medical crisis to shake me up, to make me look at one more area of my life more closely, and to live more authentically, which is to say, in a more healthy way. I discovered that I had excluded the gospel from my eating habits, but God chose to come in the way that I least expected.

The Pulitzer Prize-winning author Annie Dillard wrote a reflection on Catholic liturgy called *Teaching a Stone to Talk*. In it she expresses with both humor and forcefulness the danger in forgetting that God can come to us in alarming ways:

> On the whole, I do not find Christians, outside of the catacombs, sufficiently sensible of conditions. Does anyone have the foggiest idea what sort of power we so blithely invoke? It is madness to wear ladies straw hats and velvet hats to church; we should all be wearing crash helmets. Ushers should issue life preservers and signal flares; they should lash us to our pews. For the sleeping god may wake someday and take offense, or the waking god may draw us out to where we can never return.[1]

We are certainly more aware of the dangers of every day life than ever before. From the terrorist attacks of 9-11 to hurricanes and floods, from the credit crisis to war and unrest throughout the world, we are experiencing anxiety and instability as never before in recent memory. As Frank Rich wrote in a *New York Times* article shortly after September 11, 2001, "This week's nightmare, it's now clear, has awakened us from a frivolous if not decadent decade-long dream, even as it dumps us into an uncertain future we had never bargained for. The dream was simple; that we could have it all without having to pay any price."[2] In other words, we have been "punched down."

Unlike some other religious figures, I am not trying to point fingers and argue about cause and effect between unbridled consumerism and God "allowing" terrorist attacks,

1 Annie Dillard, *Teaching a Stone To Talk: Expeditions and Encounters* (Harper and Row, 1982) pp. 40-41.
2 Frank Rich, "The Day Before Tuesday" (*The New York Times*, September 15, 2001) sec. A, p. 23.

natural disasters or other crises. My brand of Christianity doesn't allow for such facile explanations for the mystery of human suffering. But it's clear that current events have forced us to re-evaluate our priorities as individuals, as communities and as a nation. Many of us have been questioning our own consumption of the lion's share of the world's resources and weighing it against other values, like family, relationships, spiritual growth, and personal integrity.

Having been punched down and kneaded, we don't know what shape the United States will take in the future. The nation even now is being shaped by events, by individuals and governments, by public policy and private interests. I pray that whatever shape the U.S. takes, it will also have been formed by the gospel of Christ, that Christians in positions of influence will see that justice is tempered with mercy and compassion be shown to the helpless and poor.

While I was working on this book, I spent some time at a cabin on a lake not far from the abbey, alternating between writing and baking. One day I wanted to make cinnamon rolls and realized that I had forgotten to bring a rolling pin. Some friends of mine also have a house there, so I drove over to borrow one. Tara loaned me hers and gave me some black walnuts. As I pulled out of the driveway, I knocked over their mailbox. Talk about being punched down! We laughed and laughed, and she said not to worry about it. But I felt so embarrassed that I had to bring a loaf of bread by way of apology. This whole wheat bread flavored with honey and black walnuts was the result. Tara said her family loved it, especially toasted. I've made it several times since then, and we still refer to it as "Mailbox Bread."

Whole Wheat Black Walnut Bread

Yield: 2 loaves.

2 packages active dry yeast
2 cups lukewarm water
¼ cup honey
2 cups whole wheat flour
¼ cup vegetable oil
2 teaspoons salt
1 cup chopped black walnuts
$1/3$ cup shelled sunflower seeds, toasted
3 to 4 cups bread flour, divided

Sprinkle yeast over warm water in a large bowl; stir to dissolve. Add honey and whole wheat flour; beat well, about 200 strokes. Let stand about 10 minutes, for yeast to develop. Add oil, salt, walnuts and sunflower sees; mix thoroughly. Add 2 cups of the bread flour; beat well. Work in enough of the remaining bread flour, about ¼ cup at a time, to form a soft dough; the dough will be slightly sticky because of the honey.

Turn out dough onto a lightly floured surface. Knead 8 to 10 minutes, adding small amounts of flour as needed to keep the dough manageable. Place in a clean bowl and lightly brush the surface with oil. Cover with a clean towel and let rise in a warm, draft-free place about 1 hour, or until doubled.

Vigorously punch down dough, then knead about 2 minutes. Divide dough in half and form each piece into a loaf. Place loaves in lightly greased 8½ X 4½ X 2½ - inch loaf pans. Cover and let rise about 45 minutes, or until nearly doubled.

Bake in a preheated 375-degree oven 45 to 50 minutes, or until tops are browned. Bread is done when it slides easily from the pan and sounds hollow when tapped on the bottom. Let cool on wire racks.

As individuals we are also shaped by our experience and by our choices, but ultimately the true test comes for us as it does for the bread: We must be tested by fire.

Chapter Eight
Transformed In The Fires
Of Suffering

Although we tend to take it for granted, the home oven is a relatively late development, dating from the late 1700s but not becoming common until a century later. Pioneer women on the American prairie baked most of their bread (usually cornmeal-based) on the open hearth in an iron bake-oven or Dutch oven, burying the heavy-lidded pot in the coals.

The introduction of the cookstove (as opposed to a pot bellied stove used to heat the house) made baking more popular, especially cakes and pies. But remember that these were wood-burning stoves, without dials or thermostats for regulation. Temperature was controlled by the kind of wood you burned and by how much air was let in. The standard test for baking bread was to put your hand inside the oven, and if you could stand to leave it there to the count of twenty (but no more than thirty), the oven was ready for bread baking.

Ovens have been around for centuries, of course, but they were usually communal, that is, they served the whole village or neighborhood rather than a private home. In certain parts of England, "double-decker" cottage loaves evolved, with one smaller round loaf stacked on top of a larger one to make use of the limited space in a community oven. You can still see communal ovens in the pueblos of New Mexico. Commercial bakers of the Middle Ages were required to make their ovens available to the public (for a fee) so they could bake their own bread. This custom remains today. When a Jewish friend of mine got married, his mother made use of the large oven of a local pizzeria to bake the traditional wedding *challah*.

One of the earliest mentions of an oven in Christian literature is found in the account of the death of St. Polycarp of Smyrna, a martyr of the second century. Polycarp, who was a disciple of St. John, was arrested for being a Christian and sentenced to death by fire. He was bound hand and foot and laid upon a pile of wood, which was set alight. Miraculously, the flames would not touch him but instead "billowed out like a sail." Within the flames, Polycarp's flesh appeared golden, "like bread in the oven." The terrified Roman executioner dispatched the saint by stabbing him in the throat.

St. Ignatius of Antioch also used the image of bread to describe his own martyrdom. Throughout the bishop's final journey from his see of Antioch to death in the Coliseum at Rome, he wrote letters to various Christian churches encouraging them to stand fast in the faith. In one he wrote: "I am God's wheat; I am ground by the teeth of the wild beasts that I may end as the pure bread of Christ."[1] Both Ignatius and the author of the account of Polycarp's death viewed bread as a symbol of self-sacrifice in imitation of Jesus, the Bread of Life.

Martyrdom is not required of all believers, but having some share in the sufferings of Christ is one of the conditions of discipleship: "Jesus said to his disciples, 'Whoever wishes to come after me must deny himself, take up his cross and follow me'" (Matthew 16:24). Participation in the paschal mystery (that is, in the suffering, death and resurrection of Christ) is necessary for all Christians who want to be remade in the image of Jesus. But just as dough is not instantly changed into bread, our transformation into the image of Christ

---

1 St. Ignatius of Rome, *Letter to the Romans*, 4.1, in *The Fathers of the Church*, Vol 1, "The Apostolic Fathers" translated by Francis X. Glimm, Joseph M. F. Marique, S.J., and Gerald G Walsh, S.J. (The Catholic University of America Press, Washington, D.C., 1962) p. 109.

is gradual, sometimes painfully so. *Nemo repente fit summus* wrote St. Bede the Venerable, the patron saint of our abbey: "No one is suddenly made perfect."[2]

According to St. Paul, this process of gradual transformation is made possible by baptism: "Are you unaware that we who were baptized into Christ were baptized into his death? We were indeed buried with him through baptism into death, so that, just as Christ was raised from the dead by the glory of the Father, we too might live in newness of life." (Romans 6:3-4). The Rule of St. Benedict also emphasizes that the goal is not suffering itself, but entering fully into the kingdom: "Never swerving from his instructions, then, but faithfully observing his teaching in the monastery until death, we shall through patience share in the sufferings of Christ that we may deserve also to share in his kingdom." (RB Prol.50.)

I cannot emphasize enough that "sharing in the sufferings of Christ" is not to be equated with spiritual masochism or self-hatred. In earlier generations, the desire for a share in the paschal mystery led some people to extremes of self-denial. Although they may have achieved genuine holiness by such efforts, their fervor seems excessive today. All of the teachers and spiritual directors I've known have tried to steer me away from immoderate self-discipline. When I first came to the monastery, my postulant master Fr. Herbert remarked, "Monastic life itself already has enough tests for humility without inventing any."

Fr. Herbert's point applies not only to monks but to everyone. Sooner or later, suffering comes to all of us, even if it comes to us through others—nobody's child is perfect, nobody's dad lives forever. Like the bread, we usually don't get to choose when we go into the fire. And in the same way that the heat of the oven changes smooth, white dough into golden brown crust, suffering transforms us. But here the analogy breaks down a bit, because we know that suffering

2 Bede the Venerable, *De Tabernaculo et Vasus ejus, ac Vestibus Sacerdotum*, in *Patrologia Latina* 91, 496D (Migne 1862).

doesn't have the same effect on everyone. Some people experience a personal tragedy and become embittered and cynical, others face depression and hopelessness, while others become so purified of petty selfishness and false pride that they become their true selves. Our Fr. Edmund was one in this last group.

Fr. Edmund joined Saint Bede Abbey in 1942 and after the novitiate began his studies for the priesthood. But after three years of theology he discontinued his studies when the seminary administration determined he was unable to complete the course in moral theology. In 1957, he was ordained *simplex*, that is, he was only allowed to celebrate mass at the abbey, and could not hear confessions or officiate at other sacraments.

Part of Fr. Edmund's frustration came from his struggle with alcoholism, which had plagued him from his first years in the abbey. Finally, in 1970, he successfully completed a program of rehabilitation. Shortly thereafter he undertook further theological studies, which allowed him to exercise his priestly ministry more fully.

But alcoholism had left its stamp on Fr. Edmund's psyche. Although he was active in the local AA chapter and helped many people reach sobriety, he retained some of an alcoholic's traits. Having become used to lying to cover his addiction, Fr. Edmund would often talk *around* the truth rather than being straightforward, and sometimes lied about unimportant matters. He found it difficult to hold down a job at the abbey and community members often complained about his bewildering conversations when they had to deal with him. Although Fr. Edmund was allowed to celebrate mass, his homilies were often convoluted or rambling, even incomprehensible. But he was a member of the community, and so we, his confreres, tried to accept him as best we could, although we did not always treat him with charity.

In the winter of 1986, Fr. Edmund was diagnosed with pancreatic cancer. The disease was aggressive and eventually spread to the lymphatic system; it did not respond to therapy. Father endured months of treatment and periodic hospitalization, but it was clear that the illness was terminal. By the spring of 1987, he entered the cancer ward of the local hospital for the last time.

But something miraculous happened to Fr. Edmund throughout the course of this affliction. In the face of death, he stripped away the mask he had worn for so long, and began to show us his true character. Conversations with him had a clarity and honesty that made visiting him a pleasure. Nurses knew there was little they could do for him, but they would visit him regularly and come away spiritually renewed. Sr. Kevin, a member of the hospital's pastoral care team observed, "He is the best witness we have in this hospital."

Fellow monks who visited their sick confrere returned to the monastery with inspiring stories and insights. One young monk who had his own struggles with finding his place in the community visited Fr. Edmund one evening, and as he left Father said simply, "Just be yourself, brother—I was never really good at that." On another occasion Fr. Edmund and a community member were praying the Stations of Cross (a devotion in which one meditates on the events of Jesus' suffering and death). When they got to the station in which Jesus falls beneath the weight of the cross, Fr. Edmund commented, "That's where I am right now. I want to run, I want to hurry up and die so I can be with God. But Jesus falls and says, 'No so fast, Eddy. You have to go at my pace, and I have to be with you every step of the way.'"

Fr. Edmund took great comfort in receiving daily Eucharist during his illness, but eventually he was unable to swallow. But he asked the pastoral care sister to continue to bring the Blessed Sacrament to his room. He would take the host and hold it reverently to his heart, entering a deeply spiritual communion with the Bread of Life "I am the living bread that came down from heaven," Jesus declared. "Whoever eats this bread will live forever." (John 6:51). Fr. Edmund knew this, having been fed by the Eucharist his whole life, and as that life drew to a close it nourished him still, even when he was unable to receive it physically.

When one of our brothers is in the final stages of dying, we take turns staying with him either in his monastery room or at the hospital. A few days before Fr. Edmund died, I spent the night in his room at the hospital. He had asked that the chalice and paten he had received at ordination be used as the altar vessels at his funeral mass. They were in need of a good polish, and since I was assistant sacristan at the time, I volunteered to take the night shift so I could polish the vessels and let Fr. Edmund see them.

Fr. Edmund was very weak by this point, and had a nasal tube to clear his stomach of bile, but he greeted me cheerfully and thanked me for coming. We chatted a bit about monastery news, and he dozed fitfully as I polished the silver chalice with its matching paten. When I had finished, Father asked me to bring the vessels to him. He was unable to sit up, but he set the chalice and paten upon his chest, as if he himself were the altar of sacrifice. As he held them reverently, he gave a deep sigh that was weariness and resignation and profound happiness all at once. Later as he slept I found myself haunted by the gesture, remembering another vigil, another chalice of suffering in the garden of Gethsemane: "My Father, if it is possible, let this cup pass from me; yet not as I will but as you will" (Matthew 26:39). Two days later, Fr. Edmund died.

Our transformation in the fires of suffering may not be as dramatic or intense as it was for my confrere. For some, the ordinary frustrations and setbacks of everyday life can be the "oven" of our conversion. "Martyrdom by pinpricks can be very painful," I remember reading somewhere, and I have found it to be true. Even people who appear to be successful, happy and healthy may have an interior shadow of suffering. Thomas Merton wrote that God once told him: "You will be praised, and it will be like burning at the stake. You will be loved, and it will murder your heart and drive you into the desert. You will have gifts, and they will break you with their burden."[3]

For many people in the midst of suffering, the painful heart of the matter is the question "Why?" Why do we experience suffering? Why do the innocent suffer, why do the wicked prosper, *why has God allowed this?* I am not qualified to offer rational explanations for human suffering, and I doubt anyone is. Jesus himself, an innocent man suffering an unjust death on the cross, cried out to his Father from the core of his humanity: *Why?* "My God, my God, why have you forsaken me?" (Mark 15:34). In the face of this gospel truth, we can't expect to know more than the Savior.

Jesus didn't come to take away suffering but to give it meaning. By becoming a fully human person, he united his suffering to that of the entire human race, so that when we inevitably experience pain and betrayal, we are united to God even more closely. Thus Christ's suffering was redemptive. The suffering that can separate us from family and friends draws us into closer communion with the Savior, as it did for Fr. Edmund.

In Jesus, suffering becomes inextricably linked to love. Love without sacrifice is merely affection, and he chose for himself a greater destiny. When Jesus was lifted up on the cross he gained a new perspective, and from that height he could see every person in history. He looked upon that vast sea of faces—generation upon generation of sinful, suffering, hopeful humanity—and realized that he loved them enough to die for them. And one of the faces he saw was yours.

The symbols that Jesus chose for his loving sacrifice were bread and wine. "This is my body," he said, and broke the loaf to be shared with his disciples. To be a Christian is to imitate Christ, so we next we'll look at what it means to be bread that is broken and shared.

---

3 Thomas Merton, *The Seven Storey Mountain* (Harcourt Brace, 1948) p. 422.

Chapter Nine
Blessed Broken And Shared

The next time you make toast with a slice of store-bought bread, spare a thought for Iowa salesman Otto Francis Rohwedder, who invented the first machine to slice and wrap loaves of bread. Rohwedder began working on his machine in 1912, but three years later was told by his doctor that he only had a year to live. He survived and persisted nonetheless, producing a prototype a few years later. Unfortunately, a fire destroyed his equipment, and he had to start all over.

Finally, in 1927 Rohwedder succeeded in building a plant to manufacture his bread slicing and wrapping machines, which began selling rapidly (and just in time, too—in 1926, inventor Charles Strife had received a patent for the electric pop-up toaster!). In 1928, St. Louis baker Gustav Papendick improved upon the design by placing the sliced loaves on cardboard trays to keep them neat for wrapping. By 1933, eighty percent of all bread sold in the United States was pre-sliced.

In religion class I sometimes use the expression "the best thing since sliced bread," prompting one of my freshmen to ask, "I don't get it—wasn't bread *always* sliced?" They get a longer answer than they bargained for. For centuries, I explain, bread was broken into pieces rather than sliced, making sandwiches a relatively late invention. This revelation is often met with stunned disbelief: "You mean they just tore hunks off the loaf?!" But that is precisely how people ate bread from ancient Egypt onward. Sliced bread didn't become common until people started baking it in rectangular pans rather than free form, that is, not until baking equipment became industrialized. Some bakers still consider it an insult if their baguettes are sliced rather than broken.

In the early Christian community, "the breaking of the bread" was the term used for the Eucharist, the celebration of the Lord's Supper. Even outside of a church setting, "to break bread together" signifies more than just a meal, but implies both solemnity and celebration, a feast of fellowship and unity regardless of the simplicity of the food served. When we first started making plans for a cooking show we needed a name for the series. We soon realized that "Breaking Bread" was the obvious choice for a show about baking hosted by a monk like myself, who sprinkles spiritual nuggets in between instructions for kneading and shaping loaves.

In domestic spirituality, every meal is an opportunity for Christian fellowship, but the image of a loaf broken and shared applies to the individual Christian as well. When I was in the college seminary, I read Peter G. van Breeman's insightful book *As Bread That Is Broken*. The book is about how we, like bread, are consumed in the gift of ourselves to our fellow men and women. One passage in particular has become a part of my "cookbook" for the spiritual life:

Prayer transforms me into bread that is broken. It is in the breaking of the bread that I am made available, often in ways which remain hidden to me. As bread I am given not once but many times, over and over. Prayer both demands and instills the willingness to accept this mystery as a call to which I respond with my whole being. It is in the breaking of the bread that I realize the paschal mystery of death and resurrection.[1]

1 Peter G. van Breeman, S.J., As Bread That Is Broken (Dimension Books, 1974) p 44.

My study of van Breeman's book was the first time I considered Christian service as a process of "becoming bread": a gradual, prayerful transformation of the self into the image of Christ as bread for the world. "As bread that is broken" has become a kind of mantra in my prayer, a phrase to be repeated and savored, mixed and kneaded into the dough, springing to mind at the sound of the crackle of a perfect crust.

All that sounds very romantic, doesn't it? But let's not forget van Breeman's insight that we are given "not once but many times, over and over." In other words, everybody wants a piece of us. And we'd like to give ourselves out in neat little slices—so much for him, so much for her, and here's a piece for you. But the fact is that all day people are tearing hunks out of our time and energy.

If being "broken and shared" is part of the Christian vocation, how do we keep from becoming resentful of those who ask for a "hunk off our loaf"? We have already seen in the chapter on rest that we have an obligation to take care of our own needs as well as the needs of others, which sometimes will mean saying "no" to someone we care about. But we don't always have control over how and when people will make legitimate demands on our time. How can we see these demanding moments as a blessing?

I learned a possible answer from a young woman named Tanya who attended a lecture I gave in Toledo. I was speaking about being broken and shared like bread when she raised her hand. "In the Bible," she said, "it always says that the bread is '*blessed*, broken and shared.' I'd like to hear more about being blessed first before being shared with others." I didn't have much of an answer then, but she gave me plenty to reflect on and pray about. Before we can be broken and shared, we have to be blessed.

As Tanya noted, the gospels report that Jesus blessed the bread at the multiplication of the loaves before they were broken and distributed to the crowd. He did the same at the Last Supper: "While they were eating he took bread, said the blessing, broke it and gave it to them" (Mark 14:22). My mother always makes the sign of the cross over loaves before they go into the oven, a little ritual of domestic spirituality she passed on to all of her children. If Christian service is to be "as bread that is broken," in what way can *we* be blessed before sharing ourselves?

One way is to recognize that we have *already* been blessed by virtue of having the gifts and talents that make it possible to serve people in the first place. Every once in awhile I get a bit whiney about how much work I have to do for others, but before long the Holy Spirit reminds me: "To whom more has been entrusted, more will be expected." People with the burden of ability would do well to remember that it can also be just as much a millstone to lack talents. A friend of mine in the seminary had been learning to play the organ and was asked to play for mass. "I had to tell them no," he said, "because I'm not ready." Then he burst into tears, frustrated that his inexperience kept him from using the gift he so much wanted to share. But he told me that even to be asked was a blessing in itself, because it is a sign that others at least recognized his growing gifts in music.

Another kind of blessing comes from the people around us, especially our parents and family. They bless by acknowledging our talents and encouraging us to use them. My friend Pinky once wrote to me about her family's weekly bread baking and its effect on her:

> When I was growing up during WWII we had shortages in everything. In my big family (13 under one roof) we never had enough bread, meat, sugar, etc. We baked bread on Saturdays for the week. I say "we"—actually it was my mother, uncle, & 2 aunts alternately. They made 15 loaves of white bread, then a couple of special loaves—one with raisins & cinnamon & one orange peel & walnuts. I can still remember the taste!
>
> For me and my cousins there was always a dough

allotment. We could do anything with our individual piece that we wished. It could be rolled, formed into a snake, braided, twisted, etc. I'm sure it sometimes hit the floor before it ended in a pan to be baked with the other loaves. I know it was precious to each of us & the aunts & Mom were always gracious when we offered the finished product, proudly, to be shared.

Not only did the whole process keep us occupied, but a lot of love was transferred in the process. There was learning, trust, and validation that whatever we did with love was O.K.[2]

Obviously more than just dough was being shaped in my friend's childhood home. Pinky and her cousins were being formed into confident adults by affirmation and love.

My friend's letter reminds me of a story I read in an inspirational booklet that told about the childhood of Benjamin West, who became famous for his historical paintings under the patronage of King George III of England. Having been asked to baby-sit, young Benjamin was trying to think of a way to keep his little sister Sally quiet. While his mother was out, he found some bottles of colored ink and had Sally pretend to sit for a portrait. By the time Benjamin's mother returned, there were ink blots all over the furniture. Mrs. West surveyed the mess without a word until she saw the budding artist's portrait. Picking up the picture she said delightedly, "Why, it's Sally!" Then she bent down and kissed her young son. Years later he was appointed royal painter, and became one of the most celebrated artists of his day. When asked about his inspiration as an artist, he replied without hesitation with the story of his first portrait of his sister, then added, "My mother's kiss made me a painter."[3]

In order to be open to blessings in Christian service, it helps to remind ourselves that we are not in charge of the universe, and that no matter how carefully we plan our lives,

---

2 Rosemary Riffle, letter to the author, October 31, 1994.
3 Quoted in *Our Daily Bread*, May 17, 1996.

God may have others ideas. At the end of a long media tour, my flight from Chicago to Peoria was cancelled due to weather (and you should have heard all those businessmen swear when *that* was announced!) I soon discovered that taking the bus was my only viable option. As a result I met a woman travelling home for her mother's funeral, and we had a long talk on the ride to Peoria. She didn't cry loudly or make a scene—she just needed to talk to someone and get a little spiritual guidance. Our conversation was a blessing for both of us. At the end of the trip, all I could think was: *God loved that woman so much that He cancelled that flight and ticked off all those businessmen, just to get her on a bus with a priest!*

My bus trip to Peoria gave me an opportunity to exercise two of the traditional works of mercy: to comfort the sorrowful and counsel the doubtful. Jesuit activist Daniel Berrigan writes very eloquently about the blessing one may receive from performing works of mercy, specifically to feed the hungry:

> Sometime in your life, hope that you might see one starved man, and the look on his face when the bread finally arrives. Hope that you might have baked it or bought it or even kneaded it yourself. For that look on his face, for your meeting his eyes across a piece of bread, you might be willing to lose a lot, or suffer a lot, or die a little, even.[4]

These different ways of being blessed are powerful helps on the way toward spiritual maturity, but they are not our final goal. Ultimately, Christian service is not about being blessed by others but by God. While we all deserve a pat on the

---

4 This quote came to me via a most circuitous route. Someone saw it at an exhibit on display at DePaul University in Chicago, and sent it to my friend Todd, who forwarded it to me. Subsequent attempts to find the original locus of the quote have failed, including a call to the curator of the exhibit and numerous searches by librarians and Berrigan scholars. If you can identify it, I'd love to hear from you.

back or a thank you from those we serve, we must be careful not to let our personal self-worth be bound to the opinion of others. Rather, we are valuable and precious because we are the adopted children of God, whose love surpasses that of our parents, family and friends. Further, God's love is unconditional, and therefore not dependent on the perfection of our lives or the purity of our service. "God proves his love for us in that while we were still sinners Christ died or us" (Romans 5:8). Ultimately it is God's blessing that sanctifies us, making us holy and worthy to be broken and shared in Christian service.

As is so often the case, all these reflections bring us back to prayer, which is the usual locus for receiving God's blessing. As Fr. van Breeman notes, "Prayer transforms me into bread that is broken." All Christians are blessed for service whenever they gather in the name of Christ for prayer, whether they quietly study scripture together or shout with joy as they hear a dynamic preacher or receive a prophetic commissioning during charismatic prayer. Lectio divina (indeed any form of Bible study, both public and private) is another means by which God can speak a word of blessing, through the written word of the scriptures or the silent reassurances that the Spirit utters in the heart of the believer. For Catholics, the public celebration of the sacraments is the most powerful means of sanctification for service. This is especially true of the Eucharist, where one of the usual formulas for the dismissal is "Go in peace to love and serve the Lord."

If we are unaware of the blessing and acceptance God offers us daily and depend solely upon the approval of others for our self-worth, we are destined for disappointment. This truth is demonstrated by a conversation I had with a teenage girl in a maximum security prison in Texas. I had been invited to give a bread baking lesson to a group of about twelve teenage inmates. After some initial hesitation, they plunged wholeheartedly into the dough, shaping lattice braid coffee cakes with fruit filling. Every loaf turned out beautifully, each of them as unique as the young man or woman who shaped it. At the end of the session, as we were enjoying warm bread with freshly churned butter, I asked one girl, "When they told you that you were going to make bread with a monk today, what was your first thought?" She gave a sad smile and looked down at the table: "I thought it wasn't going to turn out because I was going to make it." I wondered if she had ever been "blessed" in her young life, or if she had simply been broken, again and again, until she felt like all that was left was crumbs. I hope her success in baking was a blessing that gave her a greater sense of God's acceptance and love, and taught her that she did indeed have something precious to share with the world.

I want you to be able to have that "Wow, I did it!" feeling, to create a baked item that is both delicious and beautiful, so I'll share the recipe we used that day in the Texas prison, (the original version was in *Breaking Bread with Father Dominic 2*).

Andrew Loebach (Saint Bede Academy class of 2009) is headed for culinary school, so he comes out for baking lessons. His lattice braid looks every bit as good as mine (and yours will too).

Lattice Braid

1 pkg. active dry yeast
1 ¼ cups warm milk (100° to 110° F)
¼ cup sugar
1 Tbs. vegetable oil
1 tsp. salt
1 egg
3 to 3 ½ cups all-purpose flour
½ cup jam or preserves (not jelly)

Put warm milk into a medium size bowl. Add yeast, stir to dissolve. Add sugar, egg, salt and oil. Add 3 cups of flour and beat well. Work in enough of remaining flour to form a soft dough. Knead for 6 to 8 minutes. Rinse and dry the bowl, then oil the surface of the dough and place in the bowl. Cover with a clean, dry dish towel, and let rise in a warm place free from drafts for about one hour, or until doubled in volume. Punch dough down and knead briefly to expel larger air bubbles.

Roll dough out into a rectangle 12" x 16". In the center third of the dough, spread ½ cup of preserves or jam . Using a pizza cutter, start about ½" away from the filling and cut diagonal lines on either side of the dough at even intervals (about every 1" to 2", see illustration). Fold the strips over the preserves, alternating left and right, and tuck in the ends of the last ones to seal. Carefully lift loaf onto a lightly greased baking sheet. Cover and let rise for 45 minutes or until nearly doubled. Bake in a preheated 350 degree oven for 30 minutes or until lightly browned. Use large spatulas to remove from pan and place on a wire rack to cool. When only slightly warm, drizzle on icing and serve warm.

Icing: In a small bowl, add 2 tbs. milk or light cream, ¼ tsp. of vanilla extract and a pinch of salt to a cup of powdered sugar and stir until smooth.

No matter how much we feel blessed by God and appreciated by others, at some point or another we all feel like we've been broken and shared so much with so many people that all that's left is crusts and crumbs. In the next chapter, we'll look at the insights we can learn from leftovers.

Chapter Ten
Gather Up The Crusts

Although homemade bread often gets devoured down to the last morsel, every baker has had the experience of trying to use up leftover crusts and crumbs. After the exertion of mixing and kneading and the patience of letting the dough rise at its own pace, after carefully shaping loaves and enduring the heat of the kitchen in order to produce bread for the table, it seems a shame to let any of it go to waste. Franco Galli writes of his apprenticeship in an Italian bakery:

> At the bakery it was my job to put unsold loaves of bread atop the oven, so that they would dry for crushing into crumbs. At Bolzoni, I saw how leftover bread was used in soups, to stuff vegetables and poultry, and in pasta fillings. Bread was never wasted; it was simply transformed into another wonderful dish.[1]

In addition to the uses mentioned by Galli, leftover bread has been cubed to make croutons, mixed into meatloaf, steamed into bread pudding, sugared and caramelized to make topping for ice cream, and even used to make fresh dough. One of my creations for the first season of *Breaking Bread* was a Bread Crumb Bread, which used toasted bread crumbs

---

1 Franco Galli, *The Il Fornaio Baking Book* (Chronicle Books, San Francisco, California, 1993) p. 115.

and molasses to flavor a hearty whole wheat loaf. (It makes excellent sandwich bread and remains a favorite of *Breaking Bread* director Kent Samul.) In Tuscany they serve a bread salad called *panzanella* that is so good it will make you leave bread out on the counter on purpose.

The question of what to do with leftovers has biblical precedents as well. In St. John's version of the multiplication of the loaves, Jesus directs his disciples to "gather the fragments left over, so that nothing will be wasted." Twelve wicker baskets are filled with the broken pieces and crusts that have been produced from five barley loaves. Several commentators have suggested that the twelve baskets symbolize that the disciples are equipped to continue their ministry, even after the miracle. Nevertheless, one wonders how much bread pudding Simon Peter's mother-in-law was expected to make the next day.

Jesus' injunction to "gather up the fragments so that nothing will be wasted" was the inspiration for a program on bread baking I once presented at an adult day care center. The center was attached to a local hospital where I was a substitute chaplain, and it served adults who were not able to care for themselves fully because of age or infirmity, but didn't need the around-the-clock care of a nursing home. Usually they lived with family members who worked during the day. The clients, most of them elderly women, were dropped off in the morning and picked up again in the late afternoon or early evening. Our own Abbot Roger's mother was brought there every day by his sister. Some were recovering from surgery or strokes, others were simply suffering the effects of old age. All of them were happy to be part of a community of mutual support and genuine affection.

The nurses and aides who served at the center were among the most caring people I have ever encountered. They treated each person with dignity and patience, and arranged for activities that kept the group engaged, entertained and even educated. Birthdays were celebrated with considerable fanfare (I was once enlisted to dress up in an alligator suit for a birthday party in honor of a resident whose nickname, inexplicably, was "Alligator Joe") and staff members often brought in homemade goodies for holidays. Speakers were brought in to discuss current events, explore health issues, or, as in my case, demonstrate some craft or hobby.

I arranged to bake bread with a group of about 20 clients. Several employees raided their kitchens for mixing bowls, measuring cups and wooden spoons. While the nurses set up the work stations for crews of four people, I led the gathering in a Bible study of John's account of the multiplication of the loaves (John 6:5-13). A woman was asked to read the passage out loud, and then we discussed what it might be like to be in the crowd waiting for the bread, or how we might feel if Jesus handed us a small barley loaf and directed us to distribute it to a throng of 50 or so. Their sharing was both lively and profound—it was clear that neither age nor infirmity had dulled their spiritual insight.

Near the end of our discussion, I brought up the image of the fragments of bread as a metaphor for old age. "Sometimes older people can feel like leftovers," I suggested. "They've been broken and shared their whole lives, and it might seem like there's nothing remaining but crusts and crumbs. And our society doesn't always want to keep the crusts—sometimes people don't think the crusts are worth much and want to throw them out." Suddenly I thought I was getting too heavy, so I joked, "And that can make you feel pretty 'crummy,' can't it?" My tone was lighthearted, but as I looked around the circle of weathered faces, I saw that many of them had begun to cry.

My heart sank—after all, I was supposed to be bringing the *Good* News! I realized at that moment that I had named their pain, perhaps too well, without regard for their feelings. But as my homiletics professor once told us, you cannot help redeem what you haven't looked at fearlessly. So I continued, "But Jesus himself has said that all those crusts and crumbs should be gathered up, that you are valued, and your gifts are precious. So whatever abilities you have to share, let's bring them all together at the kitchen table and make some bread. We'll take turns measuring and mixing and kneading, and you'll each shape your own loaf to take home for supper. Whatever you can do, you can share with your group so that nobody's talents will be wasted." Much to my delight (and relief) they all smiled and burst into applause!

Before long, we had five tables of bakers organized and started distributing ingredients. I demonstrated from a table up front, promising that we could sample my loaves as our afternoon snack. The real moment of transformation came when we dissolved the yeast in warm water, and passed the bowls around for everyone to enjoy the scent. The sense of smell is of course closely linked to memory, and as soon as those ladies got a whiff of the fragrant yeast, they all became more animated and began to share stories of baking for their families and how they used to order flour by the barrel. One woman who rarely got out of her wheelchair stood up so she could mix in the flour more easily, cradling the bowl in one arm with all the authority of an experienced baker. One gentleman shared how he loved to see his mother kneading the dough at the kitchen table, her sleeves rolled up and her hair tied back with a dish towel. The room was filled with the aroma of living dough, packed to the ceiling with memory and enjoyment and love.

While the dough was rising, a staff member got out an antique butter churn, filled the glass jar with cream, and passed it around for people to turn the hand crank. Watching the fresh butter form prompted more stories about early morning milking, cantankerous cows and cold winter walks to the barn. We divided the dough and gave each participant a small aluminum bread pan in which to place his or her shaped loaf. The pans were carefully marked, placed on a cart and rolled down to the hospital kitchen for the final rise and their tour in the huge rotating oven.

The cart's return to the center's common room elicited exclamations of delight and more applause for the golden brown loaves. Mine were quickly sliced and shared, thick slices slathered with fresh butter and drizzled with honey from the abbey hives. Before long, family members arrived, expressing regret that they had come too late to share the feast but anticipating fresh homemade bread for supper. The pride in our bakers' faces shone bright as they presented their baked goods for inspection, each loaf as unique and precious and beautiful as the hands that shaped it. Abbot Roger later told me that his mother was exhilarated to be able to help feed the family again, as she had for so many years.

All of us have days when we feel we have been broken and shared until there's nothing left of us but crumbs. Sometimes after an exhausting rehearsal or a frustrating day in the classroom, I feel as though I have very little to give and can even begin to believe that I'm not really accomplishing much as a teacher, that I have "uselessly spent my strength," as Isaiah laments. But the prophet reminds us that success cannot always be measured in human terms:

> Though I thought I had toiled in vain,
>   and for nothing, uselessly, spent my strength,
> Yet my reward is with the LORD,
>   my recompense is with my God.
> For now the LORD has spoken
>   who formed me as his servant from the womb,
> That Jacob may be brought back to him
>   and Israel gathered to him;
> And I am made glorious in the sight of the LORD,
>   and my God is now my strength! (Isaiah 49:4-5).

If our reward is with the Lord, then when we feel useless and "crummy," we have to listen for Him to speak to us, to make us glorious in *His* sight, rather than worrying about outward signs of success. To do that, we have to take our exhaustion and frustration to prayer, and let *Him* be the source of our strength, rather than relying entirely on our own abilities. God has formed us from the moment of our conception, knows us through and through, with all our faults and weaknesses and failures, and still finds us precious, valued, even glorious. Although our busy schedule sometimes leaves us only the crusts of the day to offer to God, they are acceptable, to be gathered up and not wasted.

One way I keep my spirits up as a high school teacher is to save notes of appreciation from students and parents in an envelope on a table in my office. Sometimes the envelope gets covered with stacks of papers to grade or books I hope to read "someday," but I know it's there. When I start thinking that my students are coated with Teflon, so that nothing I say in class will stick to them, I get out the envelope and read a few notes. One is from an alumna who wrote to thank me for a talk I gave at senior retreat. In another, a parent wrote to express her appreciation for tutoring her son when he was failing my class (he passed, with a C+). Others are thank-you cards from kids who came for counseling or attended a mass where I preached. As I read through them, I realize that the Spirit is speaking through these letters and cards, reminding me that I have not "toiled in vain," but that my efforts really do make a difference. You might consider starting your own collection for when you feel the need to be appreciated.

Not long ago I had an opportunity to appreciate the "leftovers" from someone else's life. A friend of mine had acquired an old metal bread box from an estate sale that was filled with recipes cards, church programs and newspaper clippings. The box was roomy—a little more than a foot across, nine inches wide and just about as deep. My friend thought I might be interested in the bread recipes and so bequeathed the box to me. There were indeed plenty of recipes, but as I sifted through the large pile of papers, I discovered that what the box really held was the history of a woman's life: the crusts and crumbs of her life on the farm, in the garden, in the laundry room and especially in the kitchen.

Her name was Helen, and based on the addresses I found on a few of the papers, she lived on a farm near a small town in Illinois, the kind of town with a few houses, perhaps a small grocery store, and a grain elevator. She was frugal, and saved recipes from the labels of canned soup, clipped them from the backs of flour bags, and sometimes kept whole pages of the local newspaper from the Wednesday recipe feature. Helen collected recipes for everything, many of them written on yellowed index cards (with a fountain pen, later with a ball point) and at the top of each recipe she names the person who shared it with her. The names form a litany of friendship, lovely old-fashioned names like Florence, Cecily, Clara and Madeline. Some of the recipes are old-fashioned too, like macaroni and cheese from scratch, braised celery and watermelon pickles.

Helen was apparently active in her church; there were several programs from an Evangelical congregation. She must have been one of the best cooks in the county. Many of her recipes are the kind you'd take to a potluck: casseroles, side dishes, rolls, cakes and pies. I imagine her pastor telling her not to forget her famous green been casserole for the next Ladies' Auxiliary meeting, or a chairwoman asking if she'd bake one of her lovely angel food cakes for the mission fund bake sale.

However devoted she was to her church, her fidelity didn't keep her from having an ecumenical outlook as well. I found programs from several other congregations as well, usually when a missionary had come to speak. One page was a series of cookie recipes jotted down on the back of a mimeographed map to a nearby Presbyterian church's annual turkey dinner. When the local Catholic pastor retired, she cut out the article detailing his years of ministry and circled his new address in Florida. Helen's heart must have had a place for everyone.

Her life revolved around her family, and it's clear she knew all about domestic spirituality. Near the top of the box was a well-worn copy of *Food for the Body, Food for the Soul*, a booklet published in 1940 by the Moody Bible Institute. This publication was a small cookbook, with recipes on the left hand page and spiritual reflections on the right. Recipes for bran bread and Never Failing Biscuits were printed opposite a meditation entitled "A Spiritual Loaf." Directions for "A Scripture Cake" ("4 ½ cups of 1Kings 4:22, 1 cup Judges 5:25

. . .") were accompanied by a description of how a woman's real beauty is found in Christian character. Next to the cookie recipes there was an explanation of the symbolism of various colors of Christmas ornaments. Other reflections included "Spiritual Thoughts on Jelly Making," and a comparison of doing laundry to the process of purifying the soul. Considering the condition of the booklet (it's dog-eared and stained, and many of the recipes had comments penciled next to them), Helen must have tried to find spiritual lessons in all of her activities around the home.

Children were especially important in Helen's life, as is evident from a page on which she copied several quotations from the Bible about children and then at the bottom wrote, "What a wonderful blessing God has given us when He has entrusted us with these little ones. They are the jewels of His Kingdom." Was this a preparation for a Bible study she had to lead? Or part of her private prayer, a moment when her faith evoked a sudden rush of love that spilled out onto the page? She also saved a thank-you note from the fourth-grade class of a local grade school, thanking her for sending a treat: "We thought the cookies were 'DELICIOUS.' They were decorated very pretty." The note is dated February 16, 1955. Twenty years later she saved the label off a can of Spaghetti-O's and scribbled a memory in pencil: "Eddy said to Lois, 'We put some in a little bowl for you, Mama. January 20, 1975." Perhaps she was touched by her grandson's thoughtfulness in saving a treat for his mother, or perhaps, like most grandmothers, she simply was enchanted by everything he said. But she saved the label in an old metal bread box and left it like a treasure for me to find.

About that same time, the addresses change from a rural route to a house in a nearby small city. Did her husband die, so she had to move in with her daughter? How long did she try to hold on to her old life before she was persuaded to give up "that big old house"? Or was it easy, not wanting daily reminders of her loss—an empty chair, a silent workshop, a too-wide bed? In any case, she moved to town, brought her old bread box along, and continued to save recipes and clippings.

But more than Helen's address changed. She continued to save recipes, but many of them use boxed mixes and convenience foods. More and more there are articles about arthritis and heart disease. Several newspaper columns about the negative effects of nervous tension and depression were saved with key phrases circled and starred. In May 1978 Helen sat down to make some calculations about Social Security and Medicare, putting a column of sad figures down one side and a list of her ailments on the other: "Fatigue. Hernia. Stomach gas. Knee injury. Mental—depressed. Heart—short of breath." I also found her insurance card, perhaps the spare card she "put away someplace safe." I wonder if her daughter yelled at her when they couldn't find it, with the exasperation that can only come from watching your beloved mother transformed from caregiver to one in need of constant care herself.

Fewer and fewer recipes are saved from then onward, and only a handful of articles. One of them from 1986 shows the candidates for the Harvest Queen beauty pageant: six teenage girls' photos with a short bio of each. Was one of them a grandchild? A neighbor? An aide at the hospital during a recent stay? In any case, it is the most recent of the clippings in Helen's bread box—she folded it carefully, laid it on the top of the stack, and closed the lid for good.

Did her family even look inside before they piled the box in a crate with some old cooking utensils and few frying pans for the auction? ("Lot 27, miscellaneous kitchen items . . . what am I bid?") Perhaps it was packed away by accident, or there wasn't enough time to go through everything carefully before the sale. I believe it came to me so that the beauty of her life could be shared with as many people as possible. It's no coincidence that Helen saved all this in a bread box—it contained the crusts and crumbs of a lifetime of being blessed, broken and shared with others.

Besides, I don't believe that Helen's legacy was lost to her family. They may not have her recipe cards, but they must have their own collection of memories, especially her daughter. In the Moody Bible Institute booklet I mentioned earlier, there was a page titled "A Mother's Legacy to Her Daughter."

> WHEREAS, my daughter shall be the woman of
>   tomorrow, and
> WHEREAS, I am responsible, in a large measure, for the
>   kind of woman she shall be, I therefore bequeath to my
>   daughter the following example:

There follows a series of resolutions about the example a mother sets for her daughter: that she would remember her mother as a sincere and earnest believer in Christ; that she attended church regularly, prayed often and read her Bible; that she treated her body as a temple of the Holy Spirit; that she was a woman of good speech. Helen signed her name at the bottom, once in pencil, then a second time in pen, as if to stress the permanence of her commitment—the year was 1955. I may not know the exact year that Helen died, but I have a pretty good idea of how she lived.

And now, so do you. Helen would probably have been surprised to discover that anyone would be interested in the contents of her old metal bread box. But I find myself sorting through the leftovers of her life and wishing that we had been neighbors, that we had shared ice tea at the kitchen table and waved to each other across a backyard fence. I consider it a privilege to have her recipes—what a blessing it would have been to have her as a friend. We can only hope to spend ourselves as she did, in generosity and faith, so that when our family sifts through the crusts of our lives, someone will say, "Gather up all the fragments, so that nothing will be wasted."

I'm sure Helen shared her favorite recipes as avidly as she collected them from others. So I'll share one with you, in her honor. As I mentioned before, all the handwritten recipe cards include the name of the person who shared it with her. But one recipe in particular caught my eye. It's labeled "My Own Cookies"—just a simple oatmeal cookie with frosting (could they be the ones that were decorated so prettily for the grade school?) but evidently a recipe she developed herself and shared often with others. The next time you feel like you have nothing but crusts and crumbs to share, bake a batch for the local grade school. Be sure to save the thank-you note.

Helen's Bread Box

Helen's Own Oatmeal Cookies

Yield: About 4 dozen.

1 cup packed brown sugar
¾ cup (1 ½ sticks) butter, softened
2 eggs, lightly beaten
⅓ cup milk
1 teaspoon vanilla extract
1 ½ cups all-purpose flour
1 teaspoon baking powder
½ teaspoon salt
3 cups old-fashioned rolled oats, uncooked

Combine brown sugar and butter in medium bowl. Mix on medium speed of electric mixer until light and fluffy. Beat in eggs, milk and vanilla. Stir together the flour, baking powder and salt until well blended. Stir flour mixture into sugar mixture. Stir in rolled oats.

Drop dough by heaping teaspoonfuls onto lightly greased cookie sheets. Bake in preheated 375-degree oven 12-15 minutes, or until lightly browned. Cookies will be quite soft. Let cookies cool on baking sheet 2 or 3 minutes, then transfer to wire racks to cool completely.

If desired, frost with your favorite confectioners' sugar frosting.

In the last few chapters I have presented bread as a metaphor for our growth in faith: being punched down, shaped, transformed in the fire, blessed, broken and shared. Each of us can be bread for others, and there are hundreds of varieties of bread. In the final chapters we'll look at different kinds of bread and how they symbolize different kinds of Christian ministry.

Chapter Eleven
What Kind Of Bread
Shall We Be?

If we are to be "as bread that is broken," if we are to participate in Jesus' ministry by being broken and shared with the world, what kind of bread shall we be? I began asking myself this question when I was studying for the priesthood at Saint Meinrad School of Theology. One of my professors, Fr. Harry Hagan, O.S.B., shared with us a homily on John's account of the multiplication of the loaves, in which he compared the scarcity of food in the story to the current priest shortage. "Be bread," he had written, "be fish." He went on to mention a great variety of bread and fish—wheat, rye and pumpernickel, salmon and trout and flounder—evoking in our minds the variety of gifts, talents and temperaments found among the seminarians. He concluded with the insight that if we allow ourselves to be broken and shared, then, like the fragments of the miraculous loaves, we will be "more than when we started."

I have employed this analogy in my own ministry of preaching and teaching, often using it with high school students as a starting point for a discussion of Christian ministry, not just for priests, but for all the faithful. I usually begin by asking the students to name their favorite kinds of bread and to explain why they like them so much. We then explore how the characteristics of a particular bread can be symbolic of Christian witness and ministry. Although I've explored the analogy many times, I always receive a surprise or two from their insights—the teacher is a learner, too.

I remind them that the world is hungry; for real bread, yes—we should never forget that people go hungry every day, and we are responsible for them. To be "bread for the world" means to share our abundance with the poor. But people are hungry for all sorts of things: for affection, for companionship, for reconciliation and for forgiveness. People are hungry for affirmation and empowerment, sometimes for solitude and silence, sometimes for company. Some are hungry for knowledge, others for wisdom. Most of all, we are starving for love. Considering all these needs, how can we share ourselves? What kind of bread shall we be?

Maybe you're rye bread. Rye bread has a strong, unique flavor, but not everyone likes rye bread. So the rye bread person has a unique character, maybe even is a little bit quirky. The rye bread Christians are the prophets, the risk takers and radicals, like Francis of Assisi and Dorothy Day and the teenager who won't "join the crowd" when the crowd is clearly wrong. Not everyone is going to like that person. But the people who like rye bread *really* like rye bread. So the rye bread Christian will be just exactly what some people need in their lives; often they are exactly what the church needs, too. Don't be afraid to be a unique, one-of-a-kind, rye bread kind of Christian.

Some people are sourdough bread. As I explained in the chapter on yeast, to make sourdough starter you take a bowl of simple batter, put it out on a warm windowsill and try to capture the wild yeast out of the air. You can't see the yeast spores—you just have to trust that they'll come. The sourdough Christian works hard to create the right kind of conditions and then waits, trusting that God will provide, that something good is going to happen. The sourdough Christian lives in patience and hope.

What about cinnamon swirl bread? Cinnamon swirl toast with butter is the ultimate comfort food. You could have the worst possible day in grade school, then come home and have a piece of cinnamon swirl toast with cold milk, watch a rerun of *Mister Rogers' Neighborhood*, and life is OK again. The cinnamon swirl bread Christian is the everyday comforter: one who offers the kind word across the backyard fence, the good advice served with a glass of iced tea at the kitchen table, the squeeze of a hand, the pat on the back. Every neighborhood needs one—is it you?

Who will be our multigrain bread? Who's going to be the down-to-earth, whole-wheat, nine-grain kind of Christian witness? That kind of bread gives you fiber, something to chew on. The multigrain Christian has a lot going on inside, a whole wealth of wisdom and reflection and insight to share, like grains gathered from a dozen different hillsides. And what's the point of all that roughage? Well, there are people in this world who are spiritually constipated, people who are bound up inside somehow. They are often devout Christians who were taught that there is only one way to seek and to serve God. A little multigrain wisdom might be just what they need.

Earlier I told the story of a girl at a maximum security prison in Texas. At that same baking session, I shared this exercise with the group. One young man asked me what kind of Christian was symbolized by pita bread—something no-one had ever suggested before. Here was an 18-year-old who was in prison for a first class felony. At first glance, he looked no different than the seniors at our school; you could have stitched him into the patchwork of the Academy student body and never noticed the seam. But he looked at me with eyes that had been emptied by a hard life of bad choices, challenging me to offer him some crumb of meaning. Pita bread, I explained, is rolled very flat by the pressure of the rolling pin, then put in a very hot oven. The extreme heat causes the air and steam in the dough to expand, which forms the hollow place inside. He nodded, understanding that I was explaining more than a recipe—I wondered about the hollow spaces inside his heart, his soul. I went on to suggest that a pita bread Christian has been hollowed out by suffering, but the empty place leaves

God to fill the believer up in whatever way He chooses. I don't know whether my explanation gave him hope or not—after all, one can fill the space with junk and still feel empty. But I was grateful that he challenged me to consider the pita bread Christian hollowed out by pain and waiting to be filled with God's love.

I have a friend who is like caramel pecan rolls, a woman who pours herself out in generosity and goodness. Now just cinnamon rolls would be more than enough, but the caramel pecan roll Christian gives not only what you need, but more than you ever expected—sometimes even more than you deserve. You may have such a person at your parish or your place of business: the woman who remembers everyone's birthday, the man who offers help even before he's even asked, the one who volunteers for the jobs no one else wants. If you are blessed by the presence of such people in your life, cherish them and offer them your gratitude today. If you yourself are a caramel pecan roll Christian, thank you for teaching us how to fulfill the Lord's command: "Love one another as I have loved you."

We certainly need more pumpernickel people out there. Pumpernickel was developed during a white flour shortage, and so the baker added whole wheat and cornmeal and rye and mashed potatoes and bread crumbs and whatever else he could think of to make bread. So the pumpernickel Christians don't complain about what they don't have, they just make the most out of what they've been given and come up with something wonderful. My Grandma Tootsie was like that—having lived through the Depression, she could do wonders with leftovers and never let so much as a slice of dry toast go to waste. If you don't know any pumpernickel Christians, ask a Sunday school teacher or the faculty of your local grade school. No one knows more about working miracles on a small budget.

And raisin bread? The remarkable thing about raisins is that they keep the memory of only the sweetness of the grape. They don't recall the heat of the summer sun or the cold mornings of the harvest time. They retain no taste of the pruner's knife nor the slow process of desiccation and diminishment that transforms the round, plump grape into a small and darkened nugget. In the same way, the raisin bread Christian doesn't cling to the pain of the past but remembers what was sweetest and passes it on. Once when I shared this reflection with a group of adults at Lourdes College in Toledo, a woman said, "I know a raisin bread person," and looked fondly at her aged mother sitting nearby. Her mother's face was deeply lined with age and experience—who knows what history of suffering had been etched there? But what she had passed on to her daughter was a heritage of love; her smile showed the wrinkles that come from gratitude to God for all that had been and the expectation of joys yet to come.

Honey oatmeal bread is the bread of everyday gratitude. The honey oatmeal Christian takes nothing for granted and offers thanks for God's everyday blessings, especially those provided by the generous labor of others. Our Fr. Arthur is the abbey beekeeper, who for more than a decade has harvested and processed the honey from our apiary, some years as much as a thousand pounds of golden sweetness for the refectory tables. Unfortunately it's easy to forget that fresh honey requires wearing a bee suit in the heat and humidity of a Midwestern September. When you can see even leftover oatmeal as a sign of God's goodness, you have the makings of a honey oatmeal Christian.

One more kind of bread: banana bread (you were already thinking of it, weren't you?). You probably know how to make banana nut bread: you use the bananas that have gone bad, that are too old and spotty, too bruised to put on the table, bananas that someone else might throw away. Unfortunately, our society does that with people sometimes. We can look at others and say, "You're no good. You're the wrong color. You're too old and spotty to be of any of use. You don't belong because you are not like us." But the banana nut bread person doesn't think that way. The banana nut bread Christians go in search of the people who are bruised, the ones who seem to be going bad, the people who are a different color, the ones who are old and isolated. They seek those people out and they say, "We're going to make something special out of you. You belong here. You have a place and a purpose." And to do that, you have to be a little bit nuts. But in my cookbook, banana nut bread is the best kind of bread to be. It is the bread that Christ has called *all* of us to be.

Chapter Twelve
What Kind Of Bread Revisited

Since the publication of the first edition of *Bake and Be Blessed*, I have given the "What kind of bread shall we be?" presentation many times: at parish retreats, altar and rosary society dinners, even at a public television fundraiser. In 2004 AAA Travel invited me to lead an Alaskan cruise, and we had mass at Holy Name parish in Ketchikan. The talk was my homily, and afterwards the parish hosted us for a sourdough pancake breakfast that was better than the buffet on the ship. The Knights of Columbus at Immaculate Conception Parish in Morris, Illinois held an evening where I gave my presentation and afterwards treated the participants to a "bread smorgasbord" that featured almost every bread we discussed. A local Lutheran church invited me to speak at a soup and salad luncheon to raise money for a local food pantry; they called the event "Rise to the Knead!"

At these events, someone usually comes up with a bread that I haven't yet considered. Sometimes the Holy Spirit gives me a ready answer, sometimes someone in the assembly gets an inspiration, and other times the Spirit works through all of us as we explore the possible meanings as a group and come up with an interpretation. Naturally, I'm careful to note these new interpretations, in case I get put on the spot again! I want to share some of the ideas that have arisen over the past few years.

When I spoke at the annual convention of the Catholic Academy for Communication Arts Professionals, a woman from the South asked me what biscuits symbolize. I consider biscuits to be the bread of mystery. Either you have the gift to make biscuits or you don't (and I definitely do NOT) and in my experience no amount of instruction or monitoring will change that. They are for all appearances remarkably simple bread, but somehow their simplicity masks a unique inner quality of complexity. By comparison, the biscuit Christian has an indefinable gift to make people happy, to nourish others. On the outside they seem simple and ordinary, and yet they can minister to others when it seems no-one else can. Many who work in health care have this mysterious quality, such that simple actions like fluffing a pillow or offering a drink of water carry a special comfort. "Whatsoever you did for the least of my brothers and sisters…"

There is a bakery in the aforementioned Morris that makes exquisite potato rolls, so naturally someone brought them up as a possible kind of Christian. Potato bread is also popular in our monastery, because it's a great way to use up leftovers, and the mashed potatoes added to the dough give the bread a lovely soft texture. As it grows, the potato is nourished in the silence and dark of the earth. The potato bread Christian has nourished his or her soul in silence, grounded in peace, even when surrounded by darkness. As a result, the potato bread person can minister to others with the gentleness which is itself a kind of strength.

At Sacred Heart parish in Moline, Illinois I was asked what kind of Christian is represented by a tortilla. I confessed that I didn't have an answer, but one was provided shortly by a member of the audience. "I'm a tortilla Christian," she proclaimed proudly: "We wrap ourselves around the good stuff!" I don't think I can improve upon her answer.

It was only a matter of time before someone asked me about pizza, which happened at a bread retreat I gave at the lodge at Starved Rock State Park. Fortunately, I make a lot of pizza for my fellow monks, so I had a ready reply. The "bread" aspect of pizza, of course is the crust, which is the foundation of the pizza. A good crust is sturdy enough to handle a wide variety of toppings. So the pizza Christian is the charismatic leader who forms the basis for a diverse community. Even though he or she has a group with a wide variety of temperaments, abilities, skills and weaknesses, the pizza Christian can pull them altogether into a unified community. In our pluralistic modern times, blessed indeed is the parish with a "Pizza Pastor."

Our Fr. Ronald is an enthusiastic student of Italian cuisine, and he told me that in Tuscany they have a tradition of saltless bread, going back several centuries to when a neighboring city charged an inflated tax on salt. The Tuscans refused to be subjected to such an injustice, and developed a saltless bread instead. So those who are Tuscan bread Christians will refuse to participate in an injustice, even if their resistance costs them something. You don't have to be of Italian descent to be that kind of person; you just have to be willing to be the "salt of the earth" even when external forces try to make you "lose your flavor."

Our Jewish brothers and sisters serve a rich egg bread called challah on the Sabbath, but it must be made on Friday afternoon, so that the labor is complete before sundown and the beginning of the Sabbath rest. Inspired by their faithful example, challah bread Christians arrange their lives according to spiritual values, not the other way around. Attendance at Sunday church takes precedence over travel plans; personal integrity outweighs personal gain; daily prayer is a priority, even when it's inconvenient.

Potica is an ethnic bread much beloved by the Slovenian people, and it's popular with just about everyone in the area around Saint Bede Abbey. The monastic community receives them as gifts at Christmas and Easter, and the brethren look forward to seeing them on the holiday breakfast table. It's a bread with a filling made of honey, cream and ground walnuts. The dough is rolled out paper-thin until it covers the kitchen table, the filling is spread out, and then the dough rolled up carefully to produce layer upon layer of pastry. I consider potica to be the bread of conversion—the long spiral represents the slow process of moving toward the center which is Christ.

"What about zucchini bread?" someone piped up in a rural parish where many people grow their own produce. Zucchini bread is a great way sneak vegetables into the family diet. So a zucchini bread Christian is able to give others spiritual lessons and they don't even know they're getting good stuff, like the teacher who makes Sunday school fun, or the grandfather who imparts wisdom in every day situations. The occasion where this question arose was an ecumenical salad luncheon between the local Catholic and Methodist churches. This popular annual event is itself an example of learning the lesson of Christian unity in something as ordinary as a potluck dinner.

On several occasions I've been asked about Irish soda bread. Since my Grandma Tootsie's maiden name was McNulty, Irish soda bread is an old family favorite. Although many people seem to make this delicious quick bread only for Saint Patrick Day, I've found that it's welcome at any meal. It looks rustic and homespun on the sideboard of a farmhouse kitchen, but appears as an elegant artisan bread in fancy restaurants. In short, it's a bread that can fit in anywhere— which describes the kind of Christian it symbolizes. The Irish soda bread Christian is comfortable sharing his or her faith with anyone, and can speak to farmers and truckers and housemaids just as easily as to professionals and PhD's. The great evangelist St. Paul serves as an example. He said that in order to be able to bring people to salvation, he had become "all things to all" (1Corinthians 9:22).

Of course the other side of my family is Italian, and long loaves of Italian bread have accompanied many a meal. My Grandpa Jim was like Italian bread—crusty on the outside, but soft on the inside. You've probably met people like this, both men and women. On the surface they seem hard and unfeeling, even a bit harsh, but this crusty exterior masks a compassionate and loving heart. It might be a coach who puts the fear of God into his players, but who cares deeply about their welfare.

It might be the neighbor who yells whenever your kids' ball goes into his yard but also shovels your walk when you are sick. I've met more than one school secretary who could make principals tremble, but who showed both tough and tender love toward the student body. It has been my experience that the best way to get these crusty folk to reveal their gentler side is to hand them a baby: my Grandpa Jim turned as soft and sweet as jelly donut with a grandchild on his lap.

A boy who took my baking class at Common Threads in Chicago asked me about cornbread. To answer I gave a little history lesson about how the European settlers had to learn how to grow corn in the New World from the native peoples. The newcomers mistakenly considered the tribes to be savages, without any real civilization or worthwhile technology. And yet without the Indian knowledge of agriculture, the settlers would have starved. Cornbread is the bread of humility and respect, representing the Christian who can learn from other cultures, other traditions, even those that appear on the surface to be "inferior" to one's own. The cornbread Christian lives without judgment or arrogance, but with a simple acceptance that the Spirit can be at work in some surprising places.

I don't recall where I was when some guy asked me about beer bread, but I do remember the food event in St. Louis where there were dozens of vendors, including a booth sampling dark beer, another with sharp Colby cheese, and two nice guys selling an outstanding seasoned salt based on their mom's recipe. I developed a beer bread recipe right on the spot, sending audience members out to gather ingredients ("Go and tell them Father needs a beer!"). Ever since then I've thought of beer bread as symbolizing the Christian whose enthusiasm creates spontaneous cooperation. You've probably seen such a person at a parish meeting: maybe at the Knights of Columbus, or on the parish council, or with the school's booster club. The beer bread Christian gets a good idea for an event or activity, and his or her passion and vision spark a similar zeal in others, until the whole group is energized.

After I finished the first edition of this book, I was surprised when I realized that I had left out muffins from my reflections. What I appreciate most about muffins is their versatility, especially when I want a quick bread when a friend is coming over for coffee. I can easily adapt to my guest's tastes. For example, I have my grandmother's recipe for pecan muffins, but my guest is allergic to nuts. No problem—I can substitute raisins. If my friend loves cranberries, in goes a heaping cup with some white chocolate chips. Muffins are the bread of easy hospitality, representing the Christian who can make everyone feel welcome in her home and in her heart.

There are thousands of other kinds of bread you could be. You could be garlic bread or shortcake, you could be Scottish baps or Cornish splits. You might be challah or *kolache* or *injera*. Each of these breads has its own unique qualities, just like the unique character of each person seeking to follow Christ authentically, from the core of his or her being. Each of us is searching for balance and proportion in our lives, each of us is kneaded and punched down and shaped by the people around us, each of us transformed in the fires of suffering, each of us unfulfilled until we're blessed, broken and shared. And at the end of our lives, when all that is left is crusts and crumbs, we hope to be gathered up by loving Hands, and to discover that we are more than when we started.

Now that we have explored the many lessons bread baking has to teach us about personal spiritual growth, one question remains: What kind of bread will *you* be?

Acknowledgements

Before I became an author, I used to read the acknowledgements in other books, some of them going on for several pages. I often thought to myself: *Did you really need all that help?* The answer, of course, is a thunderous "YES!" Now that I have finished writing *Bake and Be Blessed*, I realize just how many people it takes to produce a written work, even one as simple and straightforward as this one. And so (in roughly chronological order) I express my heartfelt thanks:

- First and last, "With my whole being I sing endless praise to you. O Lord, my God, forever will I give you thanks" (Psalm 30:13).

- To Mom and Grandma for teaching me to bake, and for never kicking me out of the kitchen when they were working.

- To Abbot Martin Burne, O.S.B., for encouraging me to explore the relationship between bread and Benedictine spirituality.

- To Father Harry Hagan, O.S.B., for asking the question, "What kind of bread shall we be?" and to my freshman religion classes for challenging me to answer it.

- The unknown saleswoman at the Book House who, when I complained that there were too many bread machine books, suggested I should write my own cookbook for breads by hand.

- To Dad, for creating so many of the tools of my kitchen— I'm proud to be known as the son of a carpenter.

- To my siblings, for acting as research assistants.

- To Matt Andrew of KETC in St. Louis, for being both a trusted colleague and a good friend---none of my work in television or writing would have been possible without him.

- To Keith Dierberg and the folks at Fleischmann's Yeast, for unwavering support and sound advice.

- To Todd Schmitt, Keith Moritz, and all my student interns for *Breaking Bread with Father Dominic*, for helping me develop both recipes and reasons to bake.

- To Mr. and Mrs. Donald Davey, for providing a cabin with a kitchen and a room with a view in which to write.

- To Dan Thompson of Blue Sky Distribution, for taking a chance on an unknown monk and his recipes.

- To Terri Gates of KETC, copy editor maven and continuity queen, for insisting that my prose meet a higher standard.

- To Dr. Richard Stern of Saint Meinrad School of Theology, for challenging me to go deeper into the mystery of Christ's message and to communicate it clearly.

- To Archabbot Lambert Reilly, O.S.B. of Saint Meinrad, for encouraging my ministry and correcting my Latin.

- To Hsiao-Ching Chou, for transforming herself from newspaper interviewer to faithful correspondent and friend.

- To Pam Henderson, for sharing her expertise and her support, which are more important than she realizes.

- To Barbara Gibbs Ostmann, for honoring me by editing my recipes.

- To my confreres, the monks of Saint Bede Abbey, for testing both my recipes and my reflections, and improving both.

- To the staff at Saint Bede Abbey Press, in particular Hazel Sims, for her clear eye and unfailing cheerfulness.

- To all the Stage Rats who are willing to do dishes, wipe counters and mop floors in exchange for pizza, funnel cakes and pecan rolls.